"He called me his dad," Joe whispered as Aaron ran for the phone, eager to brag about his coolness.

Louisa turned to him and said, "Yes, he did."

Joe paused a moment, lost in the warm glow of Aaron referring to him as dad, *my dad,* then said, "Thank you."

Before he knew what he was doing, he leaned down and kissed her. It started soft and tentative, just a quick thank-you. But it slowly built into something bigger and more intense.

Her arms snaked around his neck, holding him tight, as if she didn't want to let go. The feel of her pressing against him, welcoming his touch, shook him.

"Hey," Aaron said.

They broke apart with the speed of guilty teenagers caught in the act. Louisa was blushing as she backed up, putting distance between them.

"Hey," Joe said, trying to keep it light. "It's okay if he catches us kissing. We're his parents."

Dear Reader,

The summer after my thirteenth birthday, I read my older sister's dog-eared copy of *Wolf and the Dove* by Kathleen E. Woodiwiss and I was hooked. Thousands of romance novels later—I won't say how many years— I'll gladly confess that I'm a romance freak! That's why I am so delighted to become the associate senior editor for the Silhouette Romance line. My goal, as the new manager of Silhouette's longest-running line, is to bring you brand-new, heartwarming love stories every month. As you read each one, I hope you'll share the magic and experience love as it was meant to be.

For instance, if you love reading about rugged cowboys and the feisty heroines who melt their hearts, be sure not to miss Judy Christenberry's *Beauty & the Beastly Rancher* (#1678), the latest title in her FROM THE CIRCLE K series. And share a laugh with the always-entertaining Terry Essig in *Distracting Dad* (#1679).

In the next THE TEXAS BROTHERHOOD title by Patricia Thayer, *Jared's Texas Homecoming* (#1680), a drifter's life changes for good when he offers to marry his nephew's mother. And a secretary's dream comes true when her boss, who has amnesia, thinks they're married, in Judith McWilliams's *Did You Say...Wife?* (#1681).

Don't miss the savvy nanny who moves in on a single dad, in *Married in a Month* (#1682) by Linda Goodnight, or the doctor who learns his ex's little secret, in *Dad Today, Groom Tomorrow* (#1683) by Holly Jacobs.

Enjoy!

Mavis C. Allen
Associate Senior Editor, Silhouette Romance

Please address questions and book requests to:
Silhouette Reader Service
U.S.: 3010 Walden Ave., P.O. Box 1325, Buffalo, NY 14269
Canadian: P.O. Box 609, Fort Erie, Ont. L2A 5X3

Dad Today,
Groom Tomorrow

HOLLY JACOBS

SILHOUETTE *Romance* ®
Published by Silhouette Books
America's Publisher of Contemporary Romance

To Sharon Lorei, a woman who, even if she'd chosen a
different profession, would always have been a true teacher!
I was lucky to have her for a teacher at Seneca High School...
luckier still to call her a friend.

A special thanks to Sue Herman and Pulokos Chocolate
for the inspiration!

 SILHOUETTE BOOKS

ISBN 0-373-19683-0

DAD TODAY, GROOM TOMORROW

Copyright © 2003 by Holly Fuhrmann

This edition published by arrangement with Harlequin Books S.A.

Visit Silhouette at www.eHarlequin.com

Printed in U.S.A.

Books by Holly Jacobs

Silhouette Romance

Do You Hear What I Hear? #1557
A Day Late and a Bride Short #1653
Dad Today, Groom Tomorrow #1683

HOLLY JACOBS

can't remember a time when she didn't read…and read a lot. Writing her own stories just seemed a natural outgrowth of that love. Reading, writing, chauffeuring kids to and from activities makes for a busy life. But it's one she wouldn't trade for any other.

Holly lives in Erie, Pennsylvania, with her husband, four children and a one-hundred-and-eighty-pound Old English mastiff. In her "spare" time, Holly loves hearing from her fans. You can write to her at P.O. Box 11102, Erie, PA 16514-1102 or visit her Web site at www.HollyBooks.com.

Lake Erie (5 blocks North)

The Chocolate Bar

By Design

Wagner, Chambers, McDuffy and Donovan, Law Firm

Gardner Ophthalmology

Snips and Snaps

Mabel's Acupuncture

North Park Row

East Perry Square

French St.

South Park Row

Erie, PA
Perry Square

State St.

West Perry Square

Peach St.

Five and Dime

Police Station

N

Chapter One

"Aaron Joseph, don't you dare eat that," Louisa Clancy called, but her grin took any menace from the words. "What have I told you about sneaking chocolates? You're eating my inventory."

"Ah, Mom," the boy said with all the exasperation of a seven-year-old caught in the act of pilfering treats.

"I mean it," Lou continued, resisting the urge to shake a finger in her son's face. "I'm closing the store in fifteen minutes, and then we're going home and eating dinner. You and I both know that if you've been munching chocolate, you're not going to eat a bite."

"But it was just a taste," Aaron said, defending his act of petty larceny. "I mean, this is your new chocolate. What if it's horrible? Then all your customers would go somewhere else. We'd be broke and then you couldn't buy me a new video game."

"Oh, so you're just snitching chocolate to be helpful?" she asked.

Aaron nodded his head so hard, Lou wondered how it stayed mounted on his shoulders.

She mussed his hair.

When had he gotten so big? Every time she turned around he seemed to have grown another inch. "Well, thanks for thinking of my business. Your thoughtfulness is noted, even though I suspect you're more worried about buying video games than living on the street."

Sighing at the injustice of being seven—or maybe sighing because of his failed robbery attempt— Aaron thumped his way out of the showroom and into the back room.

Louisa looked around her store, making sure everything was ready to close for the day.

Her store. The words sounded as sweet as the chocolate she sold. She'd owned it for less than a year, but already The Chocolate Bar had more than lived up to its name and its Perry Square location felt like home.

The bell over the front door chimed merrily as Lou slid an envelope back behind a stack of birthday cards.

She glanced at her watch. Five more minutes until she shut the doors. This was her last customer of the day.

She turned, plastered her business smile in place and said, "Hi. Welcome to The Chocolate Bar."

She looked up. Her smile slowly faded as she stared into piercing green eyes she hadn't seen in almost eight years.

"Joe," she whispered as she stared at the one man she never wanted to see again. Despite that fact, her heart sped up of its own accord.

"Hello, Lou. Fancy meeting you here."

Joseph Delacamp could have kicked himself.

Fancy meeting you here?

What kind of lame greeting was that?

He stared at Louisa Clancy. She hadn't changed in the past eight years. At least not much.

She still wore her auburn hair long. It was in a messy ponytail today, making her look more like eighteen than the twenty-seven he knew she was. Blue eyes darted everywhere but at him.

This was more awkward than he'd ever imagined it would be.

Not that he'd imagined walking into a candy store and running into Louisa. For years he'd imagined running into her at home in Lyonsville, Georgia, but he never had. Finally he'd simply decided she wasn't coming back. But that hadn't stopped him from thinking about her.

And now here she was.

"So, how are you?" What he wanted to ask was, *How could you?* But he didn't.

"Fine. Fine. And yourself?"

"Fine."

So polite. After all they'd shared, they were reduced to pleasant, little, meaningless social nothings.

Silence hung in the room, thick and painful.

Louisa finally broke it by asking, "So what brings you to Erie?"

"I took a job in the E.R. at the hospital. It was a great offer. Plus, you can walk outside and see the bay."

He wanted to ask if she remembered all the times they'd talked about Lake Erie, about living on its shores, about buying a sailboat and going out every evening to watch the sunset.

He wanted to ask, but he didn't. Too much time had passed, and childhood dreams were long since put away.

"So, you did it, then. You're a doctor," she said. "I'm not surprised. I always knew you could, I just wasn't sure if your parents would let you. And you're working in an emergency room. I know your dad wanted something more in keeping with the family image. A surgeon or some other impressive specialty."

"I didn't let my father live my life back in school, and that's one thing that hasn't changed." He left the underlying accusation that it was about the only thing that hadn't changed.

Louisa might look like the girl he'd known so long ago, but she wasn't who he'd thought she was back then, and he was sure she was even less like his imagined first love now.

"And you?" he asked. "Did you study marketing or advertising like you planned?"

"No. Things—" She stopped short.

Joe wondered what she'd been about to say.

"Well," she continued, "my plans changed. I came to work in Erie. I opened The Chocolate Bar last year. It's all mine. At least with the bank's help it is."

"When I came here, I never expected to find you here. After—" He forced himself to cut off any recriminations. "Well, it just never occurred to me you'd have come here. Actually, this was the last place I thought I'd find you.''

''You were wrong,'' she said with a small shrug of her shoulders.

''What made you look for a job in Erie?''

Erie, Pennsylvania.

When they were in high school back in Lyonsville, they'd sworn they wanted to leave town. They wanted to move someplace where no one knew who the Clancys or the Delacamps were. They wanted to go someplace where they could be anonymous, where no one knew their family histories three or more generations back.

They wanted a chance to be just Joe and Louisa.

Joe remember that day when, as a joke, they'd thrown a dart at a map. It had landed on Lake Erie, just beyond the Erie shoreline.

We'll move to Erie when I graduate, Louisa had said, laughing.

All these years later, he could still hear the sound of her laughter.

Despite the hardships in her life—her father had been the town drunk before he died and had left Louisa and her mother impoverished—she'd always been laughing. A quiet, joy-filled sound that had made his heart constrict even as it had made her blue eyes light up.

There was no laughter in those eyes today. Just wariness as she answered, "It's just that I always thought I'd live here. I'd spent such a long time dreaming about a Great Lake, about a place where I could just be me, not 'Clancy's kid'—you know how they used to say it with that mixture of scorn and pity in their voices. I just wanted to leave that behind."

When she'd left that behind, she'd left him behind, as well. Joe didn't understand it then, and he didn't now, but he was too proud to ask her why.

Why she'd left him when he would have followed her anywhere.

"I drove here on a whim. I drove to the foot of the dock. It wasn't as touristy then as it is now. But I stood there, and could look at the peninsula across the bay, and I knew this was home, just like I'd always dreamed it would be."

"That's how I felt, too," he said. "I'd been working at the hospital in Lyonsville, but wanted to do something different. A friend told me he knew someone who was on staff at a hospital that needed an E.R. doctor. When I checked it out and found it was in Erie, well, I knew it was the job for me, so here I am."

"Welcome to Erie." She glanced at a door toward the back of the shop, then at her watch. "But as much as I've enjoyed catching up, it's time for me to close."

"I came in to buy something for the nurses and aides in the E.R. Everyone's been so great helping me settle in, and I wanted to thank them."

"Fine, but we need to make it quick. What did you have in mind?"

She was looking at the back of the room again.

Joe looked, as well, but all he could see was a door framed by shelves, loaded with little trinkety sorts of items.

"Do you have any suggestions?" he asked.

"Would you like an assortment of chocolates? That way you're bound to have something everyone will like in the mix."

"Fine. Give me…what do you think? Five pounds?"

"Well, that would ensure that everyone got their share and then some."

"Great. Five pounds, then."

He watched as Louisa ducked behind the big glass case. She plucked handfuls of chocolate from this pile, then from that, filling up a huge box.

Five pounds of chocolate was an awful lot of chocolate. Not only could he treat the staff, but all the patients, as well.

"So this is all yours?" he asked, needing to fill up the silence.

"Like I said, it's mine and the bank's. I bought out my old boss's equipment when he decided to get out of the candy business."

She smiled when she mentioned her old boss. Joe felt a spurt of something hot. What was it?

No way could it be jealousy. He and Louisa hadn't seen each other in almost a decade. They had no claims on the other. He had no cause to be jealous.

"The lease was up on his store," she continued, "so I moved everything here. Perry Square is perfect. There are so many businesses down here, and there's been such a surge in tourism that The Chocolate Bar has done well its first year."

"I'm happy for you." He paused, looking for something else to say. "Do you ever go home?"

"No. With Mama dying six months after I left...well after that, there was nothing holding me there."

"I heard about your mother. I was sorry."

"Me, too. She'd have loved—" Louisa stopped short and stared at him a moment, then gave a little shake of her head "—to see me succeed. She always told me I could do anything I set my mind to."

"She was an amazing lady."

Louisa placed the box on the counter. "Here you go."

"How much?"

"Nothing. It's on the house."

"I can't take it without paying." He reached in his pocket and withdrew a bill and placed it on the counter.

Louisa looked ready to argue, but suddenly her eyes moved past him, and focused on something behind him.

"Hey, Mom, I'm done with my homework. Can I take a Mud Pie home, do you think?"

Joe turned around and found himself face-to-face with a boy…a boy who had his black hair and his green eyes.

"Aaron, you know better than to interrupt when I have a customer. Go into the back, and I'll come get you when I'm done."

"Geez, I just want one stupid Mud Pie," the boy mumbled as he left the room.

Joe stood, unable to move or say anything, as he tried to process what he'd just seen.

No, *who* he'd just seen.

"Louisa?" he said as he slowly turned around and faced her.

She didn't need to answer his unasked question. It was there in her face.

Guilt.

"Why?" he asked.

Why had she hidden the fact he had a son—*he had a son!*

The boy had to be sevenish, he thought, quickly doing the math in his head.

"Why?" he repeated.

Louisa was white as a sheet. "I didn't mean for you to ever know."

"That's obvious," he said. He couldn't keep the bitterness out of his voice. He didn't want to.

Even after she'd left him without a word, Joe would have sworn that Louisa would never do anything so despicable.

"I'm sorry," she said. "I know you didn't want kids—"

"You don't know anything."

"I know enough. And I'm sorry this happened. I'm sorry we rocked your nice, neat little world. You can be sure that wasn't my intention. You never wanted kids—you made that clear. I didn't plan on Aaron, but I don't regret him. He's the best thing that ever happened to me. Just walk away and forget that you saw me, forget that you saw him. Go back to the life your parents planned and plotted for you."

When they were young and talked of a future,

he'd said no children. He looked at the mess his parents and Louisa's parents had made raising children and had decided he wouldn't take the chance of following in their footsteps.

He was so young then, and all he'd wanted was the woman standing in front of him. He thought she'd known him inside and out, but if she thought he would turn away from her because she was pregnant, she'd never really known him at all.

But she was about to.

Joe needed to think. Needed to somehow find a way to breathe again. He felt as if he'd been sucker punched and there was no oxygen left in the room.

He turned to leave. Not to walk away, but to get his feet planted firmly beneath him before he tried to decide what to do next.

He just had one more question before he left. "What's his name?"

For a moment he didn't think Louisa was going to answer.

She sighed and said, "Aaron. Aaron Joseph Clancy."

She hadn't even given the boy his last name. The thought added to the pain.

He turned and walked toward the door, chocolates forgotten.

"Joe," she called. "What are you going to do?"

"I'll let you know when I've figured it out."

But figuring it out was harder than Joe could have imagined. Hours later Joe still didn't have a clue. His mind couldn't seem to focus on anything except the fact that he had a son.

Aaron.

The boy's name was Aaron.

He'd lost the first seven years of the boy's life…of Aaron's life. He felt a sense of awe and wonder every time he thought his son's name.

He made his way to the dock, though if asked he couldn't have said how he got there.

"Aaron Joseph," he whispered out loud. He didn't say Clancy. The boy should be a Delacamp.

Louisa had given the boy his name for a middle name, but that's the only thing Aaron had of his. He'd walked into the room, looked Joe straight in the eye, and there hadn't been the slightest trace of recognition.

But Joe had known. Aaron looked just the way he had at that age. All gangly, not quite grown into his body. Dark hair. And his eyes.

Aaron had his eyes.

Joe had given him physical attributes, but nothing else. Not by choice, but that didn't matter.

Joe had missed so much, so many things he should have done for and with his son.

He'd never gotten to change a diaper, never cradled him when he fussed. He hadn't seen Aaron take his first step, never kissed a boo-boo. He'd never sat up with him all night when he was sick or afraid. He'd never sung him a lullaby.

Of course, with his lack of singing ability, Aaron probably wouldn't miss that part, but Joe did. He resented the hell out of it.

The list of nevers kept growing as he sat on a bench at the end of the dock, mindlessly watching the sun sink behind the peninsula.

He hadn't taken Aaron to his first day of school, hadn't helped him with his homework. He'd never gotten to teach his son how to stand up to bullies, or how to stick up for the underdogs.

There were just too many "nevers." The endlessness of them weighed so heavily on Joe he was afraid he couldn't move under it.

Joe couldn't change the "nevers." His heart ached at the thought, but he was sensible enough to acknowledge one fact.

Joseph Anthony Delacamp had a son, and he didn't plan to miss any more of his life.

That was a promise, to himself and to his son.

* * *

"Mamma, you're sad today," Aaron said that night.

Louisa had tried to keep up the appearance of normalcy for Aaron's sake. Oh, rather than cooking dinner, she'd treated him to fast food, but that was a treat. She'd even managed to focus enough to scold him after he showered and missed a dirt smudge on his right arm.

"Soap. It's not a real shower if you don't soap all over," she'd told him.

His grumbling had felt good. It had felt normal.

But nothing else did.

Joe Delacamp had met his son today.

The thought kept intruding, inserting itself between showers and scoldings, making her stomach clench and her head ache.

"Mom?" Aaron repeated.

She'd finished reading a chapter of the newest Harry Potter book to Aaron. It was their evening tradition. She enjoyed sitting next to him, feeling his warmth and sharing the quiet time with her son.

Her son.

Not Joe's. Joe had made it clear he didn't want children all those years ago, and today, when he'd turned and seen Aaron…

"Mom? What's up?"

Joe Delacamp had met his son today.

Louisa pulled herself together and kissed Aaron's forehead. ''Nothing. I'm just tired. See you in the morning, bud.''

She walked woodenly toward the door.

''Hey, Mom?''

She turned back and drank in the sight of her son.

When he'd asked, she'd told him she'd loved his father, that they'd been young—too young to handle a relationship.

That much was true, at least as far as it went. She'd told him when he was older she would help him find and meet his father, if he wanted. He accepted her explanation and never seemed particularly bothered by the lack.

What would he think of Joe?

What would Joe would think of him?

Aaron was snuggled under the denim quilt she'd made him. It fit so perfectly with the dark-blue walls of his room. A giant poster of the planet earth was behind his head, other space pictures dotted the other walls. Aaron dreamed of being an astronaut someday, and she'd done her best to indulge him.

She wanted nothing more than for every one of her son's dreams to come true.

''Yes, Aaron?'' she asked.

''I love you.''

She held back the tears that threatened to overflow and managed to croak out, "I love you, too."

She turned off the light, and shut the door.

Joe Delacamp had met his son today.

She was still numb.

No, she was aching. There was a lump in her throat, and she thought her heart was going to break all over again.

Joseph Delacamp had come into her store today, and he'd found out he had a child. He wasn't pleased. She could see that on his face.

Maybe he was worried that she would come after him for support, or would try to make him take some interest in his son. His wife wouldn't like that. His mother would like it even less.

Well, Louisa could put Joe's mind to rest. She wanted nothing at all from him. He could keep his society wife and his society life.

Once upon a time she'd thought she couldn't live without Joe…but she'd learned differently. She wondered that she was able to keep breathing after she'd left town…left him. And yet, day after day, breath after breath, she survived.

Not that it hadn't been tough at times.

She'd moved to Erie when she was almost three months pregnant and had worked full-time throughout the remainder of her pregnancy for Elmer Shiner at his small chocolate store. Somehow she'd managed to survive her mother's death, just weeks before Aaron's birth.

Elmer had helped her through that. And he'd been the one to suggest she bring the baby to work with her, when Aaron was born.

Elmer had started out a boss and turned into her best friend. She smiled at the thought. Oh, maybe it was odd, having a seventy-year-old man as a friend, but Elmer was full of life and wisdom. He was the only father figure Aaron had ever known.

She owed him a debt she'd never be able to repay.

Everything she had, she had because of Elmer.

Aaron had never gone to day care, but had spent his first five years going to the candy store with her. He was a favorite with the customers.

When Elmer's lease on the building ran out, he announced he was ready to retire, and sold her the chocolate-making machinery at a ridiculously low price.

He'd helped her locate her new building. Helped her set up everything and get the store off the ground. He still stopped in almost every day, just to check on her and was always willing to work when she needed him.

She heard the downstairs door slam.

She rented the upstairs flat. Elmer lived in the lower one. He was home.

Joe Delacamp had met his son today.

She ran down the back stairs that connected the two apartments and knocked on the door.

"Come on in, Louie," he called.

"Elmer..." She wanted to tell him everything that had happened and tried to force the words out, but her throat constricted, and all she managed to do was cry.

"There, there, puddin'. Don't cry." He wrapped her in his arms and patted her back.

"I don't cry," she said midsob.

"What happened?" the gray-haired man said in a gruff voice. "Did something happen to Aaron?"

"No," she finally managed to say. "Not really, at least not that he knows about. His father came into the store today."

Joe Delacamp had met his son today.

Elmer let her go and stared at her. "What's he doing in Erie? I thought you left him behind in Georgia?"

"So did I. But he's here. He's working at the hospital, so he's living in Erie." She gulped convulsively. "Oh, Elmer, it's so horrible. Aaron walked into the room and Joe knew—he couldn't help but know. Aaron's the spitting image of him at seven. Joe knew and he looked furious. He's probably worried a secret son will upset the life his parents planned for him, that it will upset his perfect society wife. I don't know what he's going to do, and I'm sick with worry.''

"Now, what's to worry about? He went and got himself engaged to someone else all those years ago, despite the fact he'd asked you to marry him. So you sign some paper saying you don't want anything at all from him, make it all legal,'' Elmer said, echoing her own thoughts. "You and Aaron have got along without him this long. You certainly can manage. Just go see a lawyer and make it all legal-like, then he'll have nothing to complain about.''

"You think?'' she asked.

She needed reassurance. She'd built a wonderful, happy life for herself and her son. She didn't want Joe Delacamp to complicate it.

"Sure I think.'' Elmer patted her back. "Now, stop fretting and go get some rest. You call a lawyer. That Donovan guy across the street seems okay. At least Sarah seems to think so.'' He laughed.

Weddings seemed to be becoming commonplace within the Perry Square business community.

Libby at the hair salon had married her neighbor, Josh, the eye doctor. Then Sarah, the interior decorator who'd opened her store about the same time

Louisa opened The Chocolate Bar, married Donovan, from the neighboring law firm.

"You're right. I'll call Donovan tomorrow."

"Then call me. I'll watch the shop when you go and see him."

"Thanks, Elmer. I don't know what I'd do without you."

"Well, don't look to be figuring it out anytime soon. I plan to stick around a good long time." He paused a moment and then said, "Did I tell you I have a date?"

"No," Louisa said, knowing he was trying to change the subject, to brighten her mood. She was more than happy to allow him to. "Who?"

"You know Mabel, that acupuncturist? I was a bit nervous about dating a lady who pushed pins for a living, but she's mighty cute."

Louisa couldn't help the small smile. Mabel had been hanging out at the candy store a lot, but only on days when Elmer was there. She sensed a romance in the making. "When are you going out?"

"Next week. She asked me for this weekend, but I told her me and Aaron had plans."

"Oh, Elmer, you should have simply canceled."

"Are you kidding?" he asked. "There's a bunch of blue gill in the lake that have my name on them.

And I got tickets to some fancy-shmancy show Mabel wants to see, so it all worked out.''

"If you're sure.''

Joe Delacamp had met his son today.

Why couldn't she shake that thought?

Because Joe was in Erie.

Somewhere, right outside that window, Joe Delacamp was walking around, breathing the same air she was.

Elmer must have sensed her thoughts. He said, "I'm positive about fishing with Aaron. Now, don't you fret about that man—though I use the term in its very lightest sense. He got engaged to someone else, which means that not only isn't he much of a man, he's not very bright, either. Just call up Donovan tomorrow, and take it from there.''

Louisa felt a bit better as she climbed the stairs back up to her apartment. Of course Elmer was right. Joe hadn't wanted children eight years ago; he wouldn't want his son now.

The thought wasn't quite as comforting as it should have been. She climbed into her pajamas and went to her room. She pulled a dark-green journal from her drawer and started writing.

"Dear Joe, today you met your son—the son you never wanted....''

As she wrote, she glanced up at the eight similar

books that sat on the top shelf, above the television. She'd started a journal right after she found out she was pregnant and had bought a new one when Aaron was born. After that she bought a new journal on each of her son's birthdays.

If Aaron ever wanted to meet his father, she planned on giving them to Joe as an introduction of sorts. An introduction to a son he'd never known and hadn't wanted.

My heart froze in my chest when Aaron walked in. I saw the look of understanding dawn on your face, and then the raw, bitter anger. I wanted to tell you that I was sorry, but it would have been a lie. No matter what your mother said, I didn't plan to get pregnant, I wasn't trying to trap you. You were engaged to someone else and asked me for time. I'd have given you anything...but I didn't have time to give. Your mother was right—Aaron and I would have held you back from the life you were born to have. My only sorrow was that you'll never know what you missed.

She wrote and finally she rested. Her last thought was *Joe Delacamp had met his son today.*

Chapter Two

Joe waited outside the candy store, still uncertain what to do, what to say to Louisa.

He worked third shift last night, and was kept busy for the entire eight hours. But at the oddest time a mental picture of the boy, his son, would explode in his mind.

Aaron.

He'd whispered the name to himself, marveling in the wonder of having a son, and strangling on the knowledge that he'd missed so much.

He spotted Louisa walking down the block.

She still was one of the most beautiful women he'd ever met. The kind of woman who didn't realize how striking she was.

If all that lay between them didn't exist, she was the kind of woman he'd ask out.

Her expression when she spotted him gave none of her thoughts or feelings away. So many things about Louisa were different than he remembered, but that was probably the biggest change in her.

When they were kids he'd been able to read her like a book. Well, now the book was closed, at least for him.

He refused to speculate about whether there was another man reading her these days.

Joe met that emotionless face and wondered if maybe he'd been wrong, maybe he just thought he'd known her when they were kids.

The Louisa he'd believed in could never have done what she'd done.

"Louisa, we have to talk," he said.

"Come in," was her wooden response.

She unlocked and opened the front door and set a stack of papers down on the counter to her left.

"What do you want, Joe?"

What he wanted was to have the first seven years of his son's life back, but since he couldn't have that, he settled for asking, "Why?"

Maybe if he could understand, he could forgive Louisa.

She turned and he could see pain in her expression.

"Joe, I never meant for you to know," she said softly. "And now that you do, it doesn't change anything, if that's what you're worried about. I'm going to make an appointment with a lawyer. I'll have it all drawn up, nice and legal. Aaron and I expect nothing from you."

"That doesn't really answer my question, does it? How could you keep the fact that I had a son from me?"

"Joe, I was going to tell you, but then that announcement came. You'd just gotten engaged to Meghan."

"I explained that."

"You asked me for time.... I didn't have time to give you."

"You should have told me then."

"And what? You'd have gone against your parents, risked the business merger, broken the engagement with Meghan?"

"It wasn't real. Our parents felt the stockholders would be more comfortable merging the companies if they thought the families were merging through a marriage between us. But it wasn't real. I told you that. You should have believed me."

"I did. I believed you when you said repeatedly

you didn't want children. You had a life all planned out. I couldn't take your dreams away from you.''

"You were my dream. You know that.''

"Joe, look at you, a doctor working in an E.R. You've done everything you wanted. You accomplished your dreams. I couldn't take them away from you.''

"So you made the decision for me? You left, taking my son with you…a son I didn't even know existed.''

Louisa might have learned to hide her emotions, but Joe couldn't. He could hear the pain in his own voice, but it did little to reflect the depth of what he was feeling.

"Joe, my whys and the past aren't worth talking about. We can't change it. It's over. I know you're worried about what your wife will think, what your family will think. They never have to know. I'll have the papers drawn up and send them to you stating we have no claim on you financially. Now, if you don't mind, I have to work.''

She turned as if she was going to leave, but he grabbed her shoulder and spun her back around.

She'd shut him out by not telling him about his son, but she would never shut him out like that again.

"I do mind," he said. "We have to come to some

sort of agreement here and now. The kind of agreement that doesn't require a lawyer.''

He dropped his hand from her shoulder.

This time Louisa didn't move.

''There's nothing to agree on. Aaron's my son.'' Her voice was flat and her statement final. As if she expected him to shrug his shoulders and simply walk away from the knowledge that he had a son.

Maybe Louisa hadn't known him any better than he'd known her.

''He's my son, too,'' he said softly.

''Only in the most biological sense. You're nothing to him.''

It was a direct hit. Her remark cut at him, but rather than let her see how much, he simply said, ''That's about to change.''

Right now there wasn't much Joe was sure of— his whole world had been tilted off its axis—but he was sure that there was no way he was losing another minute with his son.

He saw that statement register and heard a faint quaver in Louisa's voice as she asked, ''What do you mean by that?''

''I want to get to know my son.''

''I won't have you coming in here, disrupting his life and then disappearing.''

''There won't be any disappearing. I plan to stick

around. I missed the first seven years of his life, I won't miss another minute. You're going to have to find a way to deal with the fact that I'm going to be a part of his life. You're going to have to share him.''

''What do you propose? Joint custody? What will your wife say to that?''

''I never married her, Louisa,'' he said softly.

He'd explained that it was just business, that he and Meghan were just friends and she'd said she understood, but obviously she hadn't. Just like he still wasn't sure he understood why she'd left.

She wasn't telling him everything. Eventually he'd get the answers he wanted, but right now he was concentrating on getting his son.

''I told you then my parents set it up,'' he continued. ''I had to wait until after the merger to get out of it, but I did get out of it. I didn't marry Meghan. I couldn't, you see. I was in love with someone else, and back then I hadn't given up hope she'd come back to me.''

She stopped a moment, staring at him, some emotion on her face that he couldn't quite identify.

''But she never did,'' he finished.

Finally she said, ''What do you want me to do? Just introduce you to him, and say, 'Aaron, by the way, this is your father and he wants to spend time with you, so you'll be bouncing from the only home you've ever known over to his place and then back again.'''

"I don't want to upset him, I want what's best for him, and I think I'm best. I am going to be part of his life. I spent the night thinking of options. I'm suggesting something better than joint custody."

"Such as?" she asked.

"Marry me."

Marry me.

When Louisa had discovered she was pregnant she'd dreamed he would say those words.

Marry me.

It's what they'd always talked about. She'd always dreamed that she would one day marry Joe Delacamp, no matter that she was just a Clancy. Just the dirt-poor, town drunk's daughter.

Then he'd gotten engaged to Meghan Whitford. A girl from his social circle. A girl he'd always claimed was just a friend.

He'd said his parents had set it up.

She'd told him to just break it off, but he'd claimed he couldn't. There was a business deal in the works and publicly breaking off with Meghan could ruin the deal.

Louisa didn't understand people who would use

something as sacred as marriage—or even just an engagement—to forge a business merger.

Joe had asked her to give him time.

Time was something Louisa hadn't had. She'd been two months pregnant with a child—the child of a man who'd always claimed he'd never be a father.

Still, despite his pseudo-engagement, she'd planned to tell him. To let him decide what he wanted to do.

And then his mother had come to her, and that one visit had changed everything....

Louisa pulled herself back from the past.

It was history.

Ancient history.

She couldn't alter what she'd done. At the time she'd thought she'd done what was best for everyone.

Now?

Listening to him talk about the son he'd never known, she wasn't sure.

"Marry me," he repeated.

"Marry you?" She laughed then, shocked at the bitterness she heard in her own voice. "You've got to be insane to think I'd marry you."

"You've got to be even more insane if you think I'm sharing custody of Aaron. I want it all. Every day. I want to be there when he gets home from school, when he goes to bed, when he gets up the next morning and has breakfast. I want to be there when he brings home his report cards. I want to hear how school went. I want to see him play—does he play sports?''

"Soccer and football," she answered.

There was a yearning in his expression. "Then I want to go to every game. I missed seven years and I don't want to miss another moment. The way I see it I have two options. I could sue for sole custody, or I can become a part of your family. Taking Aaron away from the only home and parent he's ever known is cruel. That leaves becoming part of your family. I don't think us living together—even if we're not together in a physical sense—sets a good example. That leaves marriage."

"And what if I have a significant other?" she asked.

"You'd have to break it off, of course." He paused and asked, "Do you?"

"That's none of your business."

"No, I guess it's not." Abruptly he asked, "How could you just leave me like that?"

His voice was barely more than a whisper. "I explained about the engagement. I thought you understood. And then you were just gone. I decided you were too young. After all, I was three years older than you. I figured you'd had second thoughts and were just too young, too confused to tell me, so you'd just left. But that's not why. You left to have my son in secret. Why? Did you think I'd be like my parents, trying to control him and squeeze the life out of him, inch by inch?''

''You said you never wanted children.''

''Did you think I'd abandon you and our baby?''

She could tell him about his mother's visit. She could tell him that it had been easier to just leave than risk having him agree with his parents, having him think she'd tried to trap him.

Of all the things his mother could have said, that was the one that cut to the quick.

Louisa had believed what the town said, that she was just ''that Clancy girl,'' a girl from the wrong side of the tracks.

She'd believed that people would agree with Joe's mother, that she'd tried to trap him.

She'd believed that his parents would cut him off without a dime, force him to quit school to support her and the baby, and steal his dream of being a doctor.

Maybe they could have found another way... could have dealt with all that. What others thought of her had long ago ceased to matter. But a part of her had felt that eventually Joe would believe all that as well. That he'd think she'd trapped him and stolen his dreams.

That, she couldn't live with.

What had she done?

She'd been so hurt, felt so betrayed, *been so afraid* that she'd simply left. In her heart she'd never understood how Joe could love her.

How could she have doubted him?

Looking at the pain in his face right now, she knew that he'd never have abandoned their son.

"Louisa?" Joe said. "You look like you're going to faint. Sit down before you fall down."

He led her to a chair behind the counter and helped lower her into it.

His voice was gentle, a whisper of the Joe she used to know. "Here, tuck your head between your knees and breathe deep."

She'd let her own fears and doubts rob the man she loved of knowing his son.

Slowly she sat up and fought back the tears that threatened to fall.

She should tell him. Should tell him everything that happened.

She wanted to.

She'd believed his mother and doubted Joe. She'd taken the check his mother had offered to secure her

son's future and left, thinking that breaking her own
heart was easier than waiting for Joe to break it for
her.

She hadn't trusted him enough…or trusted in
their love.

No other explanation was needed.

She'd trust him now.

It was too late for their love, but not too late for
him to know his son.

Not that she could marry him.

He said he wanted his son—he wanted Aaron—
not Louisa.

She'd thrown away their future when she left, but
she would find a way to give Aaron a future with
his father.

She'd make it work.

"The past is ancient history. Right now it's the
present we have to worry about. I have an idea,"
she said. "I have to do some checking. Meet me
after work tonight and we'll talk."

"I mean it, Louisa, I want every minute of his
life."

"I understand. And I know you don't have any
reason to believe me, but I'll do whatever I can to
see to it you and Aaron build a good relationship.
We'll talk. After work."

Chapter Three

As new man on the job, Joe worked third shift. Ten-thirty at night until six-thirty in the morning.

He should have spent the day sleeping, but instead he spent it tossing and turning.

By five-thirty, as he waited outside Louisa's store, he was a wreck.

So many questions he wanted to ask. So many details he wanted filled in.

She opened the door and looked surprised to see him there. "Joe, I thought you weren't coming."

"I said I'd be here."

"Yes, yes you did." She was quiet a minute, studying him. "Let's go over to the diner. I'll buy you a coffee."

"Is that a polite way of saying I look like I need one?"

"It's a polite way of saying you look like hell." The comment was softened with a weak smile.

"You always were direct."

"I still am."

They walked across the square to The Five and Dine.

"Cute," he said as he looked around.

It was decorated like something out of *Happy Days,* right down to a vintage jukebox.

"I like it," she said as she led him to a small booth in the back.

A waitress followed right on their heels. "Hey, Louisa."

"Hi, Missy. Could I have a coffee?"

"Sure. And you?" the girl asked Joe.

"Same." As soon as she was out of earshot, he asked, "You said something about an idea."

He needed this settled. He didn't want to waste another minute waiting to be with his son.

Louisa nodded. "I had to ask first, but..." She sighed. "There's so much we have to talk about."

"Yeah, like why you left. Why you kept my son from me. None of your explanations have answered all the questions. As a matter of fact, they just raise more. Why—"

"Joe, it was so long ago, and I've changed so much since then, but I still remember what it was like."

"What *what* was like?" he asked.

"Growing up as Clancy's kid. I remember feeling as if I'd never be more than that and wondering what you saw in me. Whatever it was you saw, I didn't see it in myself. When I found out I was pregnant, I'd never been so afraid. It wasn't that I was afraid of the baby, or even what people would say—they'd been talking all my life. I was afraid of losing you."

"Why? How could you think I wouldn't stand by you?"

The waitress brought their coffee and said, "Holler if you need something else."

"Joe," Louisa said, as soon as the woman was out of earshot, "when we talked about the future, you said repeatedly how much you didn't want kids."

"I was young and I was afraid I'd be like my parents. I thought I couldn't take the chance. But I'd never have abandoned you."

How could she have said she loved him and not known even that much about him?

"But at the time, all I knew was that I didn't measure up to you or your family and I was pregnant and you didn't want kids. I was so scared. But I planned to tell you. It took me a couple weeks to work up to it, but I'd planned it all out. We were supposed to go out that night and I even memorized what I was going to say. But then I saw the paper.''

''The engagement announcement?''

So it came back to that damned announcement?

He'd read about his engagement in the paper, as well.

His parents truly didn't see what the problem was when he'd complained vehemently about being used as a business prop. It had all fallen on deaf ears.

His parents had never seen a problem putting business before the family or, for that matter, putting appearances before feelings.

Louisa nodded. ''So I didn't say anything. Even though you explained. Don't you see, it was easier for me to believe we wouldn't make it?''

''No. I don't understand.''

She shook her head. ''Looking back, I don't either. But at the time I was young, I was afraid and I had the self-esteem of a gnat. Now? I've grown and I've learned to believe in myself. I'm stronger than you can imagine. So now I'd like to think I'd stay and fight. Then I just couldn't. It was easier to walk away than to have you say you didn't want the baby, that you didn't want me. Easier than to face the pain of having you think I'd trapped you.''

"I'd never have said that."

"But maybe, just maybe, you'd have thought it." She paused and said, "Joe, I can't undo the past. But I meant what I said, I will try to help now."

"So you'll marry me?"

He was surprised at the sense of relief he felt.

Of course, it had to do with his son, with knowing he'd be part of Aaron's day-to-day life. That's all it was. Whatever he'd once felt for Louisa was long since dead.

"No," she said, with flat finality.

"Then you're going to give me full custody of Aaron?"

"No. I said I have a third option. Move in with us."

"I won't live with you unless we're married. I might not have had much experience at this parenting stuff, but I'm sure that us living together isn't the kind of example we should set for Aaron."

"Not live with me, exactly. We live in a flat. Aaron and I are upstairs, and Elmer lives downstairs. He's got a second bedroom he says is yours for as long as you want it."

"This isn't a solution. At least not a long-term one. Unless you think I'm going to room with your friend for the next eleven years of Aaron's life." He lifted the cup as if he was going to take a drink, but

it never made it to his lips. He set it back in the
saucer with a clank.

"No, it doesn't solve anything long-term. But I
don't have any better ideas. At least not yet," she
said. "This may not be ideal, but it is a way for you
to be with Aaron every day."

It wasn't what he wanted.

Not that he wanted to sue for sole custody, either.

No, what he wanted was to marry Louisa. Not in
a white-picket-fence, minivan, buy-a-dog-and-be-a-
family, happily-ever-after sort of way. He didn't
have those types of feelings toward her anymore.

Okay, maybe he did feel something when he
looked at her, but it was only as much as any man
would feel for a gorgeous woman.

But she was right. This was a solution, at least
for now.

"When?"

"When what?" she asked, eyeing him warily.

"When would I move in?"

"This weekend. Elmer and Aaron are going fishing. I thought we could get you settled and then
break the news to him together when they get
back."

Break the news.

He didn't like her way of phrasing it. He hoped

Aaron would be happier to have him be a part of their lives than Louisa was.

He made the decision without realizing he had. "Fine. I'll need an address."

She rattled it off as he rose.

She said, "This will work for now. I do realize we have to come up with something else. Like I said, I promise to do what I can."

He didn't respond, other than to offer her a curt nod. He didn't just want to be Aaron's downstairs neighbor. He wanted to be a part of his family. That meant marrying Louisa.

This need to marry her was because of his son, he assured himself. Unfortunately the assurance rang a little less than truthful. But it was the only reason he was going to allow.

He looked at her and for a moment, like a ghost of the past, he could almost see her smiling at him, he could almost hear the way she used to laugh. But it was an illusion. She wasn't smiling or laughing now. She was waiting for him to say something.

"We're going to need to find a permanent solution soon because nothing on heaven or earth will tear me away from my son again."

She nodded, her face drawn and serious—and for a moment he caught a glimpse of her thoughts, her confusion and pain that echoed his own.

He didn't want to see anything else, didn't want any more reminders of the past. So before he could see any more he turned and walked out.

He was going to concentrate on his son.

Aaron.

He had a son, and right now that was all that mattered.

Louisa glanced nervously at the man standing next to her Sunday evening.

What was going through Joe's mind? Was he nervous? Excited?

His expression gave nothing away until the door opened and there were footsteps on the stairs.

Aaron was home, and suddenly she could see a rush of emotion play across Joe's face. Hope, anticipation…and love.

Joe loved this son he didn't know.

She felt another stab of guilt but pushed it away. The past was over and done with.

She regretted decisions she'd made, but at the time she'd done what she thought was best for everyone. All that was left to do now was deal with the present.

She had to introduce her son to his father.

Aaron rushed inside. Elmer followed at a slower pace.

"Hey, Mom, I caught ten fish. Me and Elmer—"

Aaron skidded to a halt and eyed the man standing next to her. "Hey, I know you. You were in the store the other day."

Lou hadn't introduced Elmer to Joe yet, but she saw the flash of recognition on the older man's face. Aaron had so much of his father in him that anyone would know they were father and son.

She looked at the two of them and said, "Aaron, I have something to tell you. Something wonderful."

"Yeah?" He glanced at Joe, suspicion in his eyes.

"This is an old friend of mine, from when I lived in Georgia. His name is Joe."

"Like my middle name?"

"Yes."

"Is he my fa—" Aaron let the sentence hang, as if he was afraid to say the word.

Lou wasn't sure if he was afraid Joe was his father, or if he was afraid Joe wasn't, but she smiled and nodded.

"Aaron," Joe said. "I'm so sorry that I missed so many years. Your mom and I, we were young. And we had a misunderstanding. That's not an excuse, I know, but it's all I have to offer. But I'm here now. I'm going to be staying with Elmer so that you and I will have a chance to get to know each other.''

Louisa saw the confusion in Aaron's eyes. She sank down on her knees and said, ''Your father is going to live here, with Elmer. He's going to be here every day.''

Joe sank down next to her in front of Aaron.

His hand moved forward slightly, as if he wanted to touch the boy, but he didn't.

His hand settled back on his knee and he said, ''I know you don't know me and that I have a lot to make up for. I don't expect you to believe anything I say. All I'm asking for is a chance, Aaron. A chance to be here for you. To do all the things a father should do for his son—things you've never had.''

Aaron shook his head. ''Elmer's always taken care of me and mom. We don't need you.''

''I know. But maybe I need you.''

''Honey,'' Lou said.

She reached out and placed her hands gently on Aaron's shoulder. ''I know you're confused, that you went away for a weekend and came home and found out everything changed. We both understand that. All I'm asking is you give Joe a chance.''

Aaron pulled free from her grasp. ''I'm going to my room.''

Louisa stood up. "Okay."

Aaron stalked down the hall and slammed his bedroom door.

"Well, that went great," Joe muttered as he stood as well.

"Just give him time," Louisa said. "He's just a little boy. He doesn't understand what's happened. He just knows that things have changed, and he's afraid."

"It's not change I'm afraid of," Elmer said. "What I'm afraid of is that you'll hurt my Louie again like you did before."

"She left me," Joe said quietly.

"Yes, she did, but only because—"

"Elmer," Louisa warned.

"Far be it from me to butt in…."

If things hadn't been so serious, Louisa would have laughed at that statement.

Butting in was what Elmer did best.

"But," he continued, "I will say this, boy— you're welcome to stay in my home for as long as you want or need to, but if you hurt Louisa or that little boy, you'll answer to me. I might look like an old man, but I can still take the likes of you."

"Elmer, enough," Louisa said.

She laid her hand lightly on his shoulders. Elmer

had been her best friend; he'd been the father her own had never been.

She kissed his cheek. "I'll be fine. It's Aaron I'm worried about."

"Mr. Shiner—"

"Elmer," he said gruffly.

"Elmer, I swear I'll do my best not to hurt either one of them."

Elmer stared at him a minute and then nodded. "See to it your best is enough. You had a treasure in your hand all those years ago, but you let it slip away. I hope you're a bit wiser now."

"I told Lou that the engagement was just for business," Joe said, some of the anger and pain she knew he felt slipping into his voice.

But as much as his pain cut at her, it didn't bother Elmer at all. He continued his offensive. "What kind of man would put his girlfriend in that kind of position? You kept her hidden away. You never took her to any of your family's shindigs. She was just some dark secret to be hidden from sight. And you're surprised that she left?"

"This is between me and Lou," Joe said, his jaw clenched.

"You're wrong." Elmer took another step forward, placing himself next to Louisa. "I'm her family, and I won't let you break her heart again."

"She left me."

Elmer wasn't buying that argument. "But you pushed her away."

Louisa had had enough. "Both of you, stop. I'm right here, and believe it or not, I can defend myself when and if I feel I need defending. Which I don't. Elmer, I know what I'm doing."

Elmer ignored her and stepped closer to Joe.

The older man only reached Joe's shoulder and was more than forty years his senior, but that didn't stop him from drawing himself up and repeating, "If you hurt her again, you'll answer to me."

"I don't plan on hurting her."

"You didn't plan on it last time, but you did. I saw her pain when she came into town alone and pregnant with your baby."

"A baby I never knew about," Joe said.

"A baby you didn't deserve." Elmer held up a hand. "Enough. I just want to be sure we're clear, very clear. Don't hurt her, don't hurt the boy."

"Fine," Joe said. "As long as we're speaking clearly, let me say that while I appreciate everything you did for Aaron and Louisa, and I have no desire to interfere in your relationship with them, I won't have you poisoning the relationships I'm trying to build. So I suggest we call a truce. You don't have to like me, but you do have to allow me to build something here.''

''If you don't hurt them, we'll have no problem.'' Elmer extended his hand.

Joe took it and they shook.

Men.

Strutting around like roosters in the barnyard one minute, then shaking hands like old friends the next.

Louisa didn't understand the gender at all.

''Well, I'm glad the two of you have settled that. I mean, goodness knows this poor, helpless woman needs to have you men look out for me. Why, I wouldn't have sense enough to come in out of the rain without some man telling me to.''

She glared at them. Neither had the grace to look the slightest bit chagrined.

She sighed. ''Now that you've cleared the air, let me have a bit of a say. Elmer, I love you and I know that you feel you're looking out for me, but I'm a big girl, and I know what I'm doing. The two of you will behave and will get along or I'll...''

''You'll?'' Joe asked.

''Kick your butts. And don't think I can't. I refuse to have my son grow up in a testosterone, chest-thumping house. You each had your say, and enough's enough. Now, if you don't mind, I'm going to check on my son.''

She turned and stalked down the hall.

Men.

Joe watched Lou as she left and went into Aaron's room.

He smiled.

She'd never stood up to him like that before, and despite the fact she was threatening a butt kicking, he kind of liked her ability to stand up for herself.

"Lou never used to be so…feisty," he murmured.

"*Feisty.* That's a good word for her. I think you'll find a lot of things have changed. She grew up quick—she had to. But then, she never did have much of a childhood, did she?"

"She talked to you about that?" he asked, surprised.

Louisa talked to him about her family, too, once upon a time, but never willingly. She used to say she preferred to concentrate on what she could change, rather than the things she couldn't.

As a matter of fact, that seemed to be what she was doing now…concentrating on the present and what they could do to fix things.

"She's talked to me about everything. And though she just warned me to stay out of her business, I'm going to say one more thing. That girl loved you.''

"She left me," he said again.

He still didn't understand how she could do that...how she could walk away from him and what they had, especially when she knew she carried his child.

"Ask yourself why?" Elmer said.

"Because of that stupid engagement story my parents cooked up."

Elmer shook his head. "You gotta look deeper than that, young man. A lot deeper. I'm telling you, leaving was the hardest thing that girl ever did. And knowin' how she grew up, you know that's sayin' something. If you want the whole story, you'll have to dig deeper than that.''

"I don't understand.''

"You will, if you look hard enough.''

The old man turned and walked toward the front door, then abruptly stopped and spun back around. "I meant what I said, don't hurt her. When she first got here...well, I never saw a more heartsick child. That baby, he was all that kept her going. You have a second chance here. Don't blow it.''

And with that, the old man—Joe's new room-mate—left, closing the door behind him.

Joe stood in the middle of the living room, not sure where to go or what to do.

He wanted to check on his son but knew he needed to go slow, that the boy needed time.

He thought about what Elmer had said, but he couldn't quite reconcile the picture of a heart-broken Louisa with the mental image he'd carried around all these years. He figured she'd simply brushed the dirt of Lyonsville, Georgia, off her heels and left for new places. Pretty much brushing him out of her heart at the same time.

Heartbroken?

No. He couldn't make that image mesh with the simple fact that she'd left him.

But Elmer's crack about hiding her away from his family, that one hit home.

Louisa had always claimed she didn't want to mix with his family, that she didn't want to be included in social functions. But he should have insisted. Because he didn't, it was easy for his parents to plan his mock engagement. It was easy for them not to take his relationship with ''that girl'' seriously.

That girl.

His mother always said the word with just the right hint of scorn and contempt.

That girl was going to ruin his life.

That girl was a gold digger, out to take whatever she could get.

That girl didn't fit in, would never fit in.

That girl...

After Lou left, his mother had said good riddance, and ''that girl'' was the family secret that was never referred to again. But not referring to her didn't keep Joe from thinking about her. Eight years had gone by, and yet, not a day went by that he didn't think of her at odd moments.

He'd hear someone laughing with that hint of unbridled joy, and he'd turn, expecting to see her there. But she never was.

He'd see someone with auburn hair tied back in a ponytail and for a moment—just one split second—he would think maybe she'd come back, but she never had.

And now they had a son and Elmer was telling him that he'd broken her heart.

Joe felt as if his legs had been kicked out from under him and he would never get solid footing again. In just a few short days his world had changed. He wasn't sure how to handle it.

He was still trying to puzzle it all out when Louisa came out of Aaron's room.

''How is he?'' Joe asked.

He might not understand everything going on between him and Louisa, but there was no question about what he wanted for himself and his son…he wanted a relationship. He wanted to make up for all the time they'd lost.

"He's upset. Confused."

"Can I talk to him?"

"Give him a while to adjust, okay?"

Joe nodded. "Fine. Listen, it's already six. I'm going to go to work early. I'll be home around seven in the morning."

"You don't have to leave. Aaron needs to get used to you being here, that was the point of you moving in with Elmer."

"Yes, he does. But not tonight." He turned, needing to get away.

Needing to adjust himself.

Lou touched his arm. It was the first time she'd touched him. There was the familiar jolt of connection that he'd almost forgotten. And yet, he knew whatever connection they'd once shared had long since been severed.

"Joe," she said softly. "I'll talk to Aaron. I'll try to make him see."

"Good." He turned to leave again.

"And, Joe?"

He turned back.

There were tears in her eyes.

Joe could stand almost anything but not her tears. Even after eight years he couldn't bear them.

"Don't," he whispered as he reached out to gently brush them off her cheek, as if he had the right to touch her, to comfort her. The realization that he didn't made him lower his hand, tears untouched.

"Thank you," she whispered.

"For what?"

"You could have blamed me, could have tried to make Aaron understand that this is all my fault."

"It wasn't all your fault. Don't get me wrong, I'm still angry, still feel betrayed, but I know that some of that anger is directed toward myself. We both made mistakes that led us here, to this point in time. And now we both have to work together to do what's best for our son."

"Thank you, anyway."

He just nodded, not wanting to talk right now about him and Louisa. He'd figure that all out later. Now his only concern was for his son. "I'll be home at seven tomorrow morning."

"We'll be here."

Louisa spent the night trying to comfort Aaron. He wasn't asking questions. He didn't even seem particularly happy or sad. He was just quiet, as if he was trying to readjust his reality in order to allow it to contain his father.

At bedtime she pulled out a Harry Potter book and he said, "Not tonight, Mom. Okay?"

She put the book back on the shelf and nodded.

"You know I love you, right?" she asked, needing to remind him. Needing him to know that even if the rest of his world had turned upside down, that one fact would never change.

He nodded. "I love you, too."

She kissed his forehead and left the room.

She had a million and one chores she should do, but she couldn't find the energy to face them.

Facing Joe took everything she had and then some.

So she went into her room, put on her pajamas and crawled into bed, knowing that sleep probably wasn't in the cards.

Her mind was spinning, trying to adjust to everything that happened, trying to let the fact sink in that Joe Delacamp was back in her life.

She opened the drawer of her nightstand. She took out her journal and began writing.

Page after page.

Memories of the past, how she'd felt when she'd seen Joe and, most painful of all, she wrote about how she'd made a mistake leaving all those years ago.

She was older and maybe a little wiser. And somewhere in the past eight years she'd found some self-esteem.

No, if she could go back, knowing what she knew now, she'd have never left him. She'd have stayed and fought.

But she couldn't go back and change the past.

All that was left to do was pick up the pieces and move on.

Somehow she'd make it up to Joe.

She dozed off at some point and woke up to her alarm with a start. Her journal was lying on the bed next to her, and the light was still on.

Tired, she went about her morning routine. She poured herself a cup of coffee and sat down at the table just as the back door opened. Joe came in. He was wearing hospital scrubs and looked tired.

"Good morning," she said.

"How is he?" Joe asked, the question coming so fast that she knew the worry had weighed on him all night.

"Quiet," she answered. "I don't know what he's thinking or feeling. He's just trying to work things out. All we can do is give him the time he needs and let him know we're here when he's ready to talk.''

Joe nodded. He took the seat across from her. ''Where is he now?''

''Getting dressed. He moves slowly in the morning.'' In this he was a chip off the old block. She smiled at the memory. ''If I remember correctly, mornings weren't your favorite time of day, either.''

Joe offered her a tentative smile in return. ''And if I remember correctly, you were always obnoxiously chipper first thing in the morning.''

''Still am. Guess some things never change.''

Joe shot her a look that said, *But some things do.* But he didn't say the words.

The brief moment they'd shared was gone.

''What time do you take him to school?'' he asked.

''He's got to be there by eight. I go straight from dropping him off to the store. Elmer normally picks him up at two-thirty and drops him off with me or takes him home.''

''We won't change that this week, but soon I'd like to pick him up after school. I'll go to bed right after you both leave, then get up around two.''

''Is that enough sleep for you?''

''More than enough. Residency teaches you how to get by on a lot less than six hours of sleep.''

"Okay. Not this week, but next."

"Mom," Aaron called as he came into the room. He spotted Joe and frowned. "Oh, you're here."

"Good morning to you, too," Joe said. "And yes, I'm here. I'll be here every morning and every day when you come home. That's why I moved in with Elmer, so I could be here for you."

"You weren't here last night." It was more of an accusation than a statement.

"I thought you might want some time with your mom, time to talk things over. I know you don't know me yet, but you can talk to me, too. I'll try my best to answer you."

"Do I have a grandma and grandpa?"

Louisa's heart contracted as Aaron asked the question. There was so much vulnerability in his voice.

"Yes," Joe answered slowly.

"Do they know about me?" he asked.

"Not yet."

Louisa knew that for the lie it was. Helena Delacamp knew she had a grandchild. Louisa knew she should tell Joe that part of the story. She knew that she should be honest. But she couldn't do it. It would serve no purpose.

Hearing what his mother had done would break his heart. He'd never been close to his parents, and whatever fragile relationship they'd formed, Louisa wasn't going to damage it.

She knew that Helena would never say a word and neither would she. She'd keep this one last secret from Joe in order to spare him any more pain.

He was suffering enough without her adding to it.

"Are you going to tell them about me?" Aaron asked.

"Yes. They're in Europe for a few more weeks, but when they come home, I'll tell them."

"Will they be happy?" he asked, so much a little boy. Because of his precociousness, it was sometimes easy to forget just how young he was.

"Aaron, anyone would be thrilled to find out you belonged to them." Quietly he added, "I was."

Aaron nodded.

Louisa stood. "Sit down and I'll get you some cereal, honey."

Aaron looked at the empty chair between her and Joe and continued to stand. "I think I'll get breakfast at school today, if that's okay."

"Sure. It's okay. Come on and we'll get going. We'll see you tonight, Joe."

"I'll be here." He looked at his son, and Louisa could see all the love in his eyes as he repeated, "I'll be here."

Chapter Four

Joe stirred the sauce on the stove, waiting for Louisa and Aaron to come home.

He'd made spaghetti.

And after the first hour of smelling the sauce, he knew it was a mistake.

It kept reminding him of one glorious weekend he'd shared with Louisa. They'd slipped away to his parents' cottage on the lake. He'd made spaghetti and they'd drunk a bottle of wine as they'd talked about the future.

As they'd talked about Louisa's coming graduation, Joe had asked how she felt about a small August wedding.

He had it all figured out. She would come back to school with him that fall. She'd already applied to Georgia State and had been accepted. They would set up housekeeping, go to school as man and wife.

He could still remember her joy-filled laughter as she'd jumped on his lap and kissed her acceptance up and down his face. Yes. Kiss. Yes. Kiss. Yes. Kiss.

The laughter had turned to passion. And that night, his son had been conceived.

Aaron sprang from their love.

Then things had gone wrong.

Joe slammed the lid back on the sauce and tried to do the same with the memories, slam the lid back on and hide them from sight.

The front door opened.

"We're home," Louisa called out.

Joe walked out to greet Louisa and his son.

"How was your day?" he asked, a smile pasted on his face.

He leaned down and for one split second started to kiss her cheek hello. It still felt like the natural thing to do.

She pulled away and stopped him in his tracks.

Oh, it was just the smallest movement. She stopped herself and stayed still, willing to accept his greeting. But he'd felt that initial response and it cut at him as he withdrew, maybe because he'd just been remembering another time when she'd welcomed the touch of his lips. There had been no pulling away that day so long ago.

He nodded to his son, to Aaron.

Just thinking the words *my son,* thinking Aaron's name, still gave him a thrill. He'd have preferred to pull the boy into his arms, or at the very least, to ruffle his hair. But he didn't want to force anything.

He would wait for Aaron to be ready.

"How was your day?" he asked.

Aaron frowned but did answer, "Fine."

"Good." Pretending that everything was normal, that this is how it had always been, and hoping that his son would soon realize this was the way it always would be, he said, "I started dinner. I hope you don't mind."

"Mind?" Lou said, obviously a willing player in his farce. "Why, I couldn't think of a nicer way to come home. Better watch it, I could get used to this."

"Maybe I'm hoping that's just what will happen," he said, surprised to find he meant it.

Having Lou and Aaron get used to having him here. Having them include him in their family. He couldn't think of anything he wanted more.

"It should be done in about a half hour," he said.

"Great. I have time to change."

"Want to help me with the salad, Aaron?"

The boy took a step back. "No. I got homework."

"I have," his mother corrected.

"Yeah." He took another step back. "I'm going to my room to finish."

"Sure," Joe said, forcing the smile to stay in place.

"I'm sorry," Lou whispered once Aaron had left. "It's just going to take some time." She sighed. "I bet I've said that a dozen times since yesterday."

Joe smiled. "At least. But don't worry. I'll wait for him to come around. I'm not going anywhere. I've probably said that just as often."

For a second she looked as if she was going to reach out and touch him, but she pulled her hand back. "I'm going to go change now, then I'll help with that salad, if you want."

He shrugged. "Sure."

Joe returned to the kitchen and tried not to think about the fact his son couldn't bear to be in the same room as him.

The boy was young and this was all a shock. He'd just be patient and give Aaron time to adjust, even if it killed him.

And the way Louisa had pulled away from him? He'd just been remembering a time when she couldn't wait for his touch, and now? Now was a lifetime later, and she couldn't accept his presence any more than their son could.

That would change, too.

The problem was, Joe wasn't sure what he wanted it to change into.

What did he want with Louisa? Did he simply want to reach a level of friendship with the woman he used to love, or did he want something more?

He didn't know.

"So," she said as she walked into the kitchen, dressed in a T-shirt and jeans, looking very much like the girl he used to know, "what's my assignment?"

"How about chopping the carrots?"

"Sure thing."

She got out a cutting board and walked past him. She reached out and patted his shoulder. "Give him time, Joe, he'll come around and accept you as his father."

Maybe Aaron would. But would Louisa accept his presence?

And an even harder question: Did Joe want her to?

Friday of that first week came and the situation at the house was still strained.

Louisa stood outside Aaron's classroom knowing this meeting with his teacher was necessary.

Aaron was still standoffish, not just with Joe, but with her. He wouldn't allow her to comfort him.

She was worried.

That worry increased when he brought home a math test in which he'd got a C. Aaron was a straight-A student. Even if he wasn't talking about what was happening, it was bothering him.

Quiet, withdrawn at home, and now his school-work was suffering.

If she couldn't help him through this soon, she'd have to see about professional help. She wasn't quite ready for that, but she knew it was time to talk to Aaron's teacher.

Louisa knocked softly on the classroom door. It always amazed her how different the school was once the students had been dismissed.

"Come in." Sharon Rogers called. Aaron's teacher was a delight.

Louisa had volunteered to drive for a few field trips and could easily see why Aaron loved his second-grade teacher. Bright and enthusiastic, she made school fun, not just a chore. And it was obvious that she truly loved her students.

"Thanks for staying late to meet with me," Louisa said.

She settled in the chair across from Ms. Rogers and began to explain the situation. She wasn't sure what, if anything, Aaron had said in school, and wanted the woman to be prepared.

Ms. Rogers didn't say a word. She just nodded and said, "Thanks for letting me know."

Lou had a plan and hoped Sharon would be agreeable. "You asked me to come in next week and talk to the students about the store, but maybe we should put that off for a while. You could bring the class down to the store for a tour. That way Aaron's father could come in and talk to the class about what he does. He could explain what it's like if you go to an emergency room."

Sharon reached out and patted her hand. "I think that's a wonderful idea."

Louisa was relieved.

The idea had occurred to her last night, and she hoped it would make a difference, would give Joe some common ground with Aaron. "I'm sure Joe would be willing. I'm not sure Aaron will."

"You leave that to me," Sharon said. "Aaron will ask him."

Joe had known he'd had a son for fifteen days. And for the first time he felt optimistic that someday Aaron might look on him as more than an interloper, but rather as a father. That they could develop a bond. When Aaron had asked him to come speak to his class, Joe couldn't say yes fast enough.

Now, as they walked into the store together, he looked down at the small dark-haired boy and felt a wave of love.

He practically was bursting with it.

Even after two weeks, the realization that he had a son would hit him at odd times and he'd practically drown in the wonder of it.

He had a son.

"How did it go?" Louisa asked as they came into the candy store.

Joe liked the way the store smelled. It smelled warm and comforting.

It smelled like home.

Before Joe could answer her question, Aaron burst out, saying, "Oh, Mom, it was so cool. Joe came in with a whole doctor bag full of stuff. There was a ste—"

"Stethoscope," Joe supplied.

"Yeah. And he let everyone listen to their own hearts. And his blood pressure thing. We all took turns. And then he gave everyone a mask, a real doctor mask. And stickers. And told us about what he does. Do you know that an emergency doctor is a jack…" He hesitated.

"Jack-of-all-trades," Joe said.

"Yeah," Aaron nodded, his head bobbing up and down with such speed that it was a wonder it stayed on his neck. "They do some of everything. They have to know something about all the different doctor things. It was so cool."

"It sounds cool," Lou said.

Over Aaron's head, she shot Joe a smile.

There was a flash of their old connection. That smile said how glad she was that for the first time he'd really bonded with his son.

Her gladness wasn't offered hesitantly, with worry about what a relationship between Joe and Aaron would do to her relationship with the boy. No, she gave him the smile that said having Joe and Aaron forge a bond meant more to her than anything.

He read all that in just one smile and that burst of connection.

This was the Lou he once knew, the girl he'd once loved.

No not a girl. She was a woman now.

"...and Joe said sometime maybe we could go down to the hospital and he'd take me to the cafeteria and show me around."

"Sure, that sounds great," she said.

"They have an ice cream machine in there, and Joe said I could get some."

"Sure you can."

"Listen, I gotta go call Mark, okay? He thought he was so cool 'cause his dad drives trucks and they have a zillion gears. But I said my dad gets to cut people open and see their guts. That's cooler."

"Guts are certainly cooler than gears," Lou said. "You may go in the back room and call Mark."

"He called me his dad," Joe whispered as Aaron ran for the phone, eager to brag about his coolness.

Louisa turned to him and said, "Yes, he did."

"Thank you."

"For what?" she asked.

"Ms. Rogers said you stopped in last week and explained the situation."

"Of course I did. I just wanted her to know what was going on in case Aaron started to have trouble in school."

"That's not all she said. She said that my going in today was your idea, that you thought it would be good for Aaron and me."

Louisa shrugged. "And it was good for you both."

"I know. He called me his dad."

Joe paused a moment, lost in the warm glow of

Aaron referring to him as dad, *my dad,* then repeated, ''Thank you.''

Before he knew what he was doing, he leaned
down and kissed her. It started soft and tentative,
just a quick thank-you. But it slowly built into something bigger and more intense.

Her arms snaked around his neck, holding him
tight, as if she didn't want to let go. The feel of her
pressing against him, welcoming his touch, shook
him.

''Hey,'' Aaron said.

They broke apart with the speed of guilty teenagers caught in the act.

''Yes?'' Joe asked, surprised to find his voice still
worked after what he'd just shared with Louisa.

''Mark wants to know if he can come over and
play with your stethoscope?''

''Sure,'' he said. ''Anytime. I'd like to meet your
friends.''

''Cool,'' he exclaimed and ran into the back
room.

Louisa was blushing as she backed up, putting
distance between them.

''Hey,'' he said, trying to keep it light. ''It's okay
if he catches us kissing. We're his parents.''

''Yes, we are.'' Her tone was flat and Joe couldn't
read her.

That fragile moment shattered. The fact that she was once again closed to him brought home just how much of a stranger she was.

She'd been kind and true to her word, trying to help him get to know Aaron. Sometimes it was easy to forget how much things had changed, but then something reminded him all over again that Louisa wasn't the girl he'd once loved.

"It's just this is where I work. I need to be professional. And Aaron's never seen me with someone like that," she continued.

"Never?" Joe asked.

He'd spent that first year without Louisa dating everyone and anyone, looking for someone to replace what he'd lost. But he'd never found it.

He'd never felt a tenth with any of those women what he felt right now, simply kissing Lou.

Why was that?

One answer tried to push its way out, but Joe firmly tamped it back down. He was here, practically living with Louisa for Aaron's sake.

Nothing more.

Nothing less.

Whatever they had was over.

But a small question had been tugging at his thoughts for a while now... Could they find something else, something new together?

"No other man," she said.

"You mean you never brought your dates over to the house?" he asked.

"Dates?" She laughed and started fussing with a rack of chocolates in the case. "Who had time to date?" she asked, without looking up.

Actually, after that first wild year when he was so hurt, so angry with Louisa and had dated frequently, his social life had become rather sparse. With medical school, then his residency, there hadn't been time.

"It's been eight years," he said. "Certainly you've dated."

"Sure. I can count them on one hand."

She held up her right hand, and with her left, pushed down three fingers. "Elmer's nephew Thomas comes to town once a year to visit. He's taken me out to dinner three times. Of course, all we do is talk about Elmer. Thomas would like him to move to Seattle, but Elmer says Erie's home, so Thomas checks up on him with me. No kissing involved at all. Just friendly conversation."

She pushed down the remaining two fingers. "And then two times I dated this lawyer guy who frequented the store, back when I was working for Elmer. I guess I should have been suspicious about a guy who needed to buy that much chocolate, but

I was naive. Let's just say that I wasn't interested in the type of relationship he wanted.''

She sighed. ''Five. Five dates in eight years. Not a great average, is it? I'm sure you had scads of women after you and Meghan broke it off.''

He didn't want to address the ''scads'' part, but was tired of hearing about Meghan. ''How many times do I have to tell you that there was never anything between us other than friendship. We'd known each other forever. Her parents were as obnoxious as mine. We shared that. We were friends. But only friends.''

''Except for that brief stint as fiancés,'' she pointed out.

''I explained it all then. That was my parents' doing. Not mine.'' He raked his fingers through his hair, wanting, no needing, to make her understand. ''It was just business.''

''I guess I'm just a simple girl. I don't understand that kind of business. Just like I never understood why you were with me.''

''What you were—what you always were—was special. You humbled me.''

She laughed, but there was no hint of the girl he once knew in that laughter. It sounded almost bitter.

''I'm serious,'' he said, his voice softening as the anger left him. ''I know what it was like for you when your father was alive, but you never hung your head. When people talked about him, you just faced them with that look.''

"What look?'' she asked.

"The one that said, 'I can't help who he is, but I'm not him. I'm nothing like him.' You wore your dignity around you like a mantle, and no one could miss it.''

"And yet, I was still just Clancy's kid.'' She looked away. "No matter how much dignity I had, I was still just the town drunk's daughter.''

Joe took her chin in his hand and forced her to look at him. "Not to anyone who knew you. To them you were just Louisa. A proud, amazing girl. And though so many things have changed, that's one thing that hasn't. You're still amazing. What you did for me today…''

"I didn't do anything. You did it,'' she said.

"But thank you, anyway.''

"You're welcome.''

She looked uncomfortable, so he changed the subject.

Today they were celebrating. His son had called him Dad.

"I want to ask you about something.''

Just then the door opened and a trio of women walked into the store.

"See, I told you Louisa had a man in here," the gray-haired woman announced.

Three sets of eyes stared at him.

The gray-haired woman stepped forward. "I'm Pearly. Pearly Gates. My mama used to say that my name was the closest to heaven I was ever going to come because I had way too much of the devil in me to reach such lofty heights. She was a Southern lady, quiet and discreet. Me, I don't beat around the bush. So, who are you and why are you in here kissing Louisa?"

The redhead cleared her throat and Pearly turned. "Oh, the bubble-popper, she's Josie. We work down the street at Snips and Snaps. The other woman, she's Mabel. She's a needle sticker with a shop around the corner."

"Needle sticker?"

Mabel shot Pearly a sharp look, then turned back to Joe and said, with dignity, "I'm an acupuncturist. And though I can work miracles, I don't think even I have a chance at reining in Pearly."

"Like I'd let you stick me," Pearly said with a snort of laughter. "Now, you know who we are. Who are you?"

"Joe. Joe Delacamp."

He looked at Louisa, hoping for some clue as to who these women were and what, if anything, they should be told. She didn't move a muscle, but he could see her permission in her eyes. "I'm Louisa's…friend."

"Now, I know I'm not as young as I used to be," Pearly said, "but I don't think I'm ready for hearing aids just yet. You two seem a bit closer than *friends.*"

"Pearly," Louisa said, "Joe's Aaron's father."

"Well, I'll be a burr on a bear's behind. For almost a year, the three of us have been trying to set you up, and now you go and bring this tall, dark, mysterious man out of your closet."

Pearly turned to the other women. "She was obviously pining for him all this time, which is why our matchmaking didn't work."

"Oh," the other two women chorused.

"Now, I'm not going to ask you two for any more particulars," Pearly assured them, "but I will say, you should have told us."

"I—"

"So when's the wedding?" Pearly asked.

"Wedding?" Louisa choked. "There's not going to be a wedding. Joe's here because of Aaron. Nothing more, nothing less."

"And that kiss?" Pearly asked, slyly.

"It was just… It didn't mean…"

Joe waited, hoping Louisa could explain away

that kiss, because he couldn't. He didn't have a clue why he'd kissed her.

What they had so long ago was over. All that was left was their bond through their son. But that type of bond didn't require kissing, and Joe felt as if he definitely did require kissing…kissing Louisa again soon.

"Well then, girls," Pearly said, rubbing her hands together with obvious anticipation, "we might not have fixed our Louisa up, but it would appear that the Perry Square Business Association is about to have another party to welcome her boyfriend to town."

"We've got the pizza party coming up. We can introduce her boyfriend around then," Mabel said. "Then when they get married, we'll have a good and proper reception for them."

"Joe's not my boyfriend. And there's not going to be a reception or a wedding," Louisa said, though the three women were busy chattering to themselves and were ignoring her.

"Weddings seem to be becoming a habit." Josie emphasized the statement by blowing a huge bubble with her gum, then snapping it loudly. "I wonder when Mr. Right will find me?" She sighed.

"There's not going to be a wedding," Lou said, louder this time.

"Well, I've got my Elmer," Mabel said. "We're going out again this weekend."

"Speaking of that," said Pearly to Mabel. "Did you know about this and not tell us?"

"No. Elmer doesn't gossip, more's the pity," Mabel said. "I'm sure he knew Louisa would tell us in her own time."

"All right," Josie said with a nod. "So, about a reception. You know these things take time to plan."

"There won't be a reception," Louisa said with force. "There won't be a reception because there's not going to be a wedding. Joe and I don't feel like that about each other."

"So, you kiss men you don't care about?" Pearly asked.

"No. I…we…Joe, help me out, would you?"

"Ladies, it's such a pleasure to meet Louisa's friends," he said, rather diplomatically.

Then suddenly, out of the blue, he heard himself say, "And Louisa's right, there's not going to be a wedding, but not because she wasn't asked."

He couldn't believe he said it, but the reaction of the three women was almost worth the angry look that Louisa shot him.

"You asked her to marry you?" Josie said with a huge sigh. "That's so romantic."

"Oh, honey, that's sweet," Mabel crooned.

"Joe!" Louisa yelled.

"Oh, I'm going to get Elmer for not filling me in on any of this," Mabel muttered.

Pearly was the only quiet one. She stood there studying Joe. "So, you asked her to marry you?"

"Yes. I should have done it years ago. Well, actually, I did ask her years ago, but I made a mistake. A big one. Maybe if I'd been smarter then, we wouldn't have wasted all this time."

"Smart man," Pearly said with an approving nod.

"Not a smart man, a dead man," Louisa muttered.

"Are you going to come to our pizza party and let me introduce you around?" Pearly, ignoring Louisa's obvious distress, asked Joe.

"I'll be there. I'd love to meet the rest of Louisa's friends."

"But—" Louisa's protest was silenced when Pearly pulled her into a warm embrace.

"Now, the boy has the right idea. Even if you said no, and won't marry him, he should know your friends. After all, as Aaron's father, he'll be a part of your lives even without a marriage."

"And a reception," Josie added. "I really like receptions."

"But—"

"Did I ever tell you of my cousin Fancy Mae Stump?" Pearly asked.

Josie and Mabel both groaned.

Louisa shook her head. "No. I'm pretty sure I'd remember a name like Fancy Mae Stump."

"Well, Fancy Mae had a fancy name, but unfortunately she had a rather stumplike quality. All the Stumps—they were my mother's cousin's kids— were short and stocky. We always thought their mama gave them such pretty names to make up for the fact they were destined for stumpyness."

"Oh, no, here she goes again," Josie muttered, then blew the biggest bubble that Joe had ever seen, popping it as a sort of punctuation to her sentence.

Pearly shot the redhead an annoyed glare, cleared her throat loudly, then continued. "Now, where was I?"

"Fancy Mae," Mabel supplied.

"Right. Well, Fancy Mae met Milton Hedges at a barn dance at the Coopers' farm one summer." She stopped a moment, then said, "Did I ever tell you about the Coopers' prize hog, Garner?"

"No, but you know the rule, one story at a time," Josie said. "As a matter of fact, the new rule should be one story a day…that's all anyone should have to bear."

"Bear? Why I'll have you know—"

"Fancy Mae," Mabel said, interrupting the potential squabble.

"Yes, well she met Milton and danced with him all night but didn't seem to realize he was interested in her. She told my mama that he probably was just pleased to find a woman willing to overlook the wart on the end of his nose."

Looking pleased with herself, Pearly folded her arms over her chest and looked back and forth between Joe and Louisa.

Finally Louisa said, "Uh, Pearly, I know you always have a moral to your stories, and maybe I'm being dense, but I don't see this one's."

"Why, it's as plain as the wart on the end of Milton's face…he didn't dance with Fancy Mae because she was convenient, or even willing. He danced with her because he liked her. After he convinced her that he really liked her despite her stumpyness, they both realized that the likin' wasn't all there was, there was lovin' too. They married and had a bunch of warty, stumpy kids and you never did see such a happy family."

"For pity's sake, Pearly, no one sees a moral in that," Josie said.

Pearly sighed a put-upon sigh and said, "Louisa's Joe wasn't just kissin' her 'cause they were old friends, or even because they have a son. Why, it's as clear as the wart on—"

"—Milton Hedges's nose that they still have feelings for each other," Mabel finished for Pearly and punctuated the sentence with a huge sort of girly gaga sigh that would have sounded more at home coming from a teenager than from a woman so many years his senior.

Pearly smiled, obviously pleased. "Right you are."

She turned to Joe and Louisa, "Talk to you soon. Nice meeting you, Joe. I'm looking forward to getting to know you."

"Uh, same here, ladies," Joe said weakly.

He felt as if he'd been caught up in a whirlwind, and as the three swept out of the store, he felt himself fall back to earth with a thud.

"And that," Louisa said weakly, "was the heart of the Perry Square Business Association. Your arrival will be up and down the square in less time than it takes me to wrap a box of candy."

"I'm part of your life now, Louisa. Your friends would have to know sometime."

"Yes," she said without much enthusiasm.

"Does it bother you?"

"Of course not," she said quickly, almost too quickly.

"Because you don't look happy."

"I'm a private person, I don't—" She stopped short and then changed the subject. "You were going to talk to me about something—something that sounded serious—before they walked in."

"Yes, I was. Come on, let's sit down." He led her to the couch she kept over by the cards.

He let her sit down first, then sat right next to her, rather than on the other end of the couch.

If he'd sat down first, he knew his thigh wouldn't be pressed against hers right now. She'd be as far away as possible.

Maybe it was time to change that.

Aaron was still his primary concern, but the more time he spent with Louisa, the more he realized that he still wanted her. And that desire grew with each passing day. It pressed against his chest making it hard to breathe when she was around.

And yet, how could he want someone he couldn't trust?

"You wanted to ask me something?" she prompted.

He forced himself to concentrate on the question at hand. Later, when he was away from her and could think, he'd reflect on this need and how to address it.

"It's about Aaron," he said. "One of the kids in

his class commented on the fact that my name is Delacamp, and his is Clancy. I'd like to have his last name legally changed. He's a Delacamp.''

"I didn't want to suggest it, but I've thought about it,'' she said.

That surprised him. "You've thought about it?''

"Joe, I didn't give him a name for a week after he was born because I couldn't decide what was right. What was fair. Finally I used my last name just because I thought it would be easier for him.''

"I thought you wanted to forget he was a Delacamp, just like you'd forgotten me,'' he admitted.

"I never forgot you, Joe. Believe what you will of me, but don't believe that. I thought about you every day. I wondered about you. I almost called you so many times.''

"Then why didn't you? I was beating myself up worrying about you, wondering what I'd done. And then, as the pain receded, there was anger. I was furious that you'd left me like that, without a word.''

"I'm so sorry, Joe.'' She laid a hand gently on his forearm. "We keep coming back to this. We keep circling back to the past, to the whys and the recriminations. I am so sorry. There's no excuse. I was young. I was scared.''

That small touch made him hungry for more, but instead of pulling her into his arms, he managed to ask the question that had been plaguing him. "Did you really think I'd desert you and the baby?"

"No. No, I was more afraid that you wouldn't, and that you'd resent us a little more each day. That the resentment would grow and that one day you're going to realize what I'd known all along—that I wasn't good enough for you, that I didn't belong with you and never would, no matter what I did. You would think I'd trapped you and that I'd ruined your life and shattered your dreams."

"You were my dream," he practically whispered, once again trying to reassure her.

"But in the end, I might have been your nightmare. I was too afraid to let that happen, so I ran. And I am sorry."

He was about to argue, to let her know that would never have happened, but she held up her hand.

"Joe," she said, her voice clogged with emotion. "I can't talk about this anymore right now. About Aaron's last name—I think we need to leave it up to him, but I think it would be good."

"Then we'll talk to him. Together," he said.

They would talk to their son, but Louisa wouldn't talk to *him*.

She got up and left the showroom, disappearing into the back area. He didn't follow her.

Not good enough?

Is that really how she'd felt?

That day Elmer had mentioned how he'd kept Louisa hidden away and hadn't included her in family events. He thought she hadn't wanted to be included, but looking back, he could see how she might interpret it as a sign that she was inferior, something to be kept out of sight.

How could he explain that he'd wanted to keep her separate from his family, from that world, not because he was ashamed of her but because she was too good for them?

What a mess.

With sudden clarity he realized he wanted more than to live on the fringes of Louisa and Aaron's life.

He wanted so much more.

What he'd felt for Louisa all those years ago hadn't died at all. What he felt now wasn't exactly the same. Back then he'd loved her with all the intensity of a young man just coming into his prime.

And now? What he felt was different. He wasn't sure just what it was, but it was something.

He loved the way she was with Aaron.

He'd walked in on her talking to Elmer a couple of times, and she'd sounded like the old Louisa…laughing, bubbling over with enthusiasm for their son, for her store.

He wanted her to talk to him like that.

He'd made the first step in gaining his son's affections, but he hadn't made much of any progress with his son's mother.

He hadn't even realized that he wanted to make progress until now, until this moment. But there it was, so clear and intense he couldn't believe he'd missed it before.

He cared about Louisa.

It wasn't just some leftover feelings from their past. It was something new and different. It was something he wanted to explore.

Slowly he was chipping away at her, discovering things he'd never realized back in Lyonsville. But he still wanted better answers than she'd given him, because maybe if he understood, he could trust her again.

And maybe, maybe, if he could trust her, they could start something new, something real.

Chapter Five

"Do you have plans this afternoon?" Joe asked Louisa Saturday at breakfast.

It was *his* breakfast, she reflected. For the rest of the world, it was somewhere between lunch and dinner.

Three weeks.

He lived with Elmer…well, at least slept at Elmer's. But the rest of the time he was here.

She was getting used to having him around and couldn't decide if that was a good thing or not.

"No. Not real plans. Saturdays are when Aaron and I try to get all the household chores done and take care of the shopping and stuff. We did everything except the vacuuming. Why?"

She'd hoped by now things would be less awkward. And maybe they were, at least between Joe and Aaron. But she felt things were decidedly more awkward between her and Joe.

He made her…nervous.

Every time she turned around, there he was. Since that kiss at her store, he hadn't touched her and she was…relieved. Of course that little sizzling sense of attraction she felt for him was just some leftover girlhood crush. Or maybe it was simply a grown woman's attraction to a good-looking man.

She could deal with it. And she was relieved that he hadn't kissed her again.

The fact that she'd dreamed about that kiss— dreamed about it every night—meant nothing.

She realized Joe was speaking as she sat fantasizing about kissing him.

"…and I'd like to go."

"I'm sorry." She'd missed what he'd said entirely. "Where did you want to go?"

"The peninsula. I know it's too late in the season for swimming, but it's warm enough to just spend the day on the beach. I think it might be fun." He paused and then added, "I haven't been there yet and I'd like the first time I go to be with you."

Louisa's initial reaction was a sort of quick affirmative. His comment about going with her gave her a warm, melty sort of feeling.

And because she wanted to say yes, she'd have to say no.

Absolutely not.

She had enough memories of the past bombarding her. She didn't want to deal with a dream from the past, as well. Going to the peninsula with Joe was so close to what they'd dreamed of, and yet the situation they were in was miles away from what they'd planned.

After that dart had landed on Erie they'd read everything they could find on the city, and of course that included information about Presque Isle State Park. It comprised a natural peninsula that stretched out into Lake Erie and provided the city with its bay. She could quote the facts, list them all, and still the fact remained—she didn't want to go with Joe.

"Are you sure you want to go today? It's already almost four and it gets dark so much earlier these days," she said, hoping he'd change is mind.

"It's just in time for a dinner picnic. We can watch the sunset. Besides, I don't think Erie has many more nice weekends coming its way, does it?"

"No," she said, knowing her fate was sealed.

"So? I think Aaron would enjoy it, don't you?" he pressed.

Yeah, sure Aaron would enjoy it. But would she?

"Yes, he would." She knew when to admit defeat. "We spent a great deal of time there during the summer. It was kind of you to think of inviting us."

"I wasn't being kind, Lou," Joe said. There was the faintest hint of annoyance in his tone.

"I didn't mean to upset you," she said.

"You didn't," he said, then stopped. "Okay, maybe you did a little." He smiled.

Louisa felt some of the tension in her chest ease at the sight of his slightly crooked grin.

"It's just," he continued, "I want us to be a family, not just three people sharing a living space. Doing things together. That's what a family does."

"Not mine." Unless you counted the times she went with her mom to find her father and drag him home. That was what constituted the Clancy family togetherness.

"Nor mine. But I'm pretty sure I read it someplace. Or maybe I saw it on some talk show."

It was a truce and Lou accepted it with a laugh. "Ah, you watch talk shows?" She tsked. "It's a terrible vice."

"Before I came here, there were a lot of hours to fill. Talk shows kept me company."

She touched his hand. "I'm sorry."

"Don't be. I'm here now. And I want to see if the talk shows are right about families, that spending time together can be fun."

He turned his hand and stroked the inside of her palm.

She pulled her hand away as if his touch burned.

Actually being burned might be less painful.

She folded her arms across her chest and nodded. "Okay."

He stood, grinning. "Let me have a shower and we'll go."

"I'll go get Aaron," she said.

"Where is he?"

"Out back with Elmer."

"Tell you what, you find him, I'll get dressed and we'll stop at Taco Bell for our picnic. You always liked Mexican food."

Lou laughed. "There's one right on Peninsula Drive. I bet I can still outeat you when it comes to tacos."

"We'll just see about that," he said with a chuckle as he started to leave to get ready.

He turned. "Hey, Lou?"

"Yes?"

"Thanks."

His gratitude about such a small thing left her choked up. Each time she saw how hard he was trying with Aaron, the thought that she'd denied him his son for so long cut at her.

She couldn't undo the past, she reminded herself for the umpteenth time. But she could work with the future and make sure Joe and Aaron got all the time they needed to build a close relationship.

To build the kind of family that she and Joe never had…a talk show kind of family.

It was perfect, Joe thought as he sat on a blanket next to Louisa. Aaron was running around on the beach, tossing a loaf of stale bread to the seagulls, piece by piece.

She sat next to him, close but not touching.

An almost overwhelming urge to reach out and wrap his arm around her kept pulsing through his body, but he resisted, sure she wouldn't welcome his touch and wishing more than anything that she would.

"Mom," Aaron suddenly screamed. "It's almost time."

He ran the short distance that separated him from the blanket and plopped down between Joe and Lou.

His thigh brushed against Joe's, and Aaron didn't pull away.

That one small touch warmed Joe's heart. Aaron was adjusting to him. The boy wasn't calling him Dad, but he'd referred to him as "my dad" a couple of times. Each time was like a gift, and Joe was warmed.

"Look, it's almost happening."

"What is happening?" Joe asked, not that he cared. What mattered was he was here with Louisa and his son. It was a talk-show-family kind of moment.

"The sun's going to hit the water in a minute," Aaron said.

"Oh."

He turned. "Don't you know the story?"

Joe shrugged. "Afraid not."

"When the sun hits the water, you can hear it hiss if you listen hard enough. Whenever Mom and I come out we listen, but we've never quite heard it. I almost did once, but then a bunch of seagulls started squawking for more bread. That's why I quit feeding them early today. Maybe they'll be quiet and we'll finally hear it. Have you ever heard it?"

Joe shook his head. "No, but where I lived there wasn't a big lake like this one."

"I know. It's so big, it's like an ocean. You can

sit here and believe that it really is the end of the earth. That's what Mom says.''

''What else does Mom say?'' Joe asked.

Louisa's eyes met his over their son's head, and she glared at him.

She was annoyed he was pumping Aaron for information on her.

Joe could live with her annoyance.

She was avoiding talking to him just as much as she was avoiding touching him. And if she wouldn't talk, Joe had learned enough about his son in the past few weeks to know Aaron would.

Talking was one of the things Aaron did best.

''We sometimes go out back at home and watch the stars. Mom says each star is a wish. She's got one special one—it hangs right over the big tree out back. I asked what that wish was, but she said it was one that would never come true. But she likes to look at it and think about what it would be like if it had.''

Joe had a wish like that. A wish he'd never thought would come true, and yet here he was, sitting on the beach with it...with them.

''Shh.'' Aaron said. ''Here it goes.''

Joe noted that they all three moved forward slightly, as if they might hear the hiss if they were closer.

The sun sank in all its pink-hued glory and touched the water.

"Did you hear it?" Aaron whispered.

"No. Sorry," Joe said. "Did you?"

"Nope. But there was that little bit of wind. It probably blew the hiss back into the water."

"Probably."

"Maybe next time. Mom says, There's always next time." He sprang up, grabbed the rest of his bread and ran back to the seagulls.

"Is that right?" Joe asked Louisa.

She turned her head toward him, but her eyes didn't meet his. "Is what right?"

"That there's always next time?" Joe asked softly.

"Yes," she said softly. "At least when it comes to sunsets."

"And what about us?" he asked, though he hadn't meant to.

The discovery that he still had feelings for Louisa—even though he wasn't sure what they were—was building in his chest, like a balloon pressing against his ribs, just aching to get out.

"What about us?" she asked, inching away from him.

"Is there a chance that this time—our next time— we can get it right?"

"Do you want to?" she asked softly.

"To be honest, I don't know what I want. When you left, it just about killed me. And when I found you in the shop that first day…I don't know how to explain all the emotions. There was an initial sense of elation that you were there. And as I realized that you'd been in Erie all this time, a sense of, I don't know quite what it was, but it was warm. The thought that you'd come here just like we'd planned… It made me happy. I would have asked you out to dinner, would have wanted to catch up and see if we could reconnect. And then…" he paused.

"And then Aaron came in," she supplied.

"It was like a physical blow. I had a son. You'd had him all this time and I'd never known. I was furious, I was heartbroken."

"I'm sorry," she said softly. "I can't tell you how sorry. I keep saying it and I mean it. If I could go back, if I could undo it, I would."

"It wasn't just you I was mad at. It was me. I went along with my parents' ruse. And Elmer said something the other day—"

"Joe, I'm sorry. Elmer shouldn't have said anything. I've warned him, but warning Elmer doesn't always work. I'll talk to him."

"Don't be sorry. He was right. I should have in-

sisted that you get involved with my family. He said
I hid you away.''

"No, no you didn't,'' she said. "I didn't want to
go to your family functions. I knew how they felt
about me.''

"I should have insisted that they accept you,'' he
said.

"You can't force people to accept each other.
And, Joe, this was my fault. I should have trusted
you. I should have told you.''

"But—''

"We can't do this. We keep coming back to this,
coming back to a past neither of us can change.
Maybe we both made mistakes. We've both apolo-
gized, and that's that. We can't beat ourselves up
over the past. We could spend the rest of Aaron's
childhood arguing about whose mistakes were the
biggest ones, but it wouldn't get us anywhere.''

"So, we're back to the question, what do we do
with this second chance?'' he said softly.

"I'd like to think we could learn to be friends
again. I missed that. A hundred times a day I'd see
something or hear something and think, *I've got to
tell Joe*. Even now, before we met again, every now
and then something would happen and my first
thought was telling you. And every time I realized
I couldn't, it was like right after I left, the pain.''

He held out his hand. "Friends?"

She hesitated a split second, and he wasn't sure she was going to take his hand, but she did.

Her hand felt warm in his.

Warm and right.

"Friends," she said. "It was where we started before. Maybe with time we can trust each other and find something new."

She gently pulled her hand out of his.

Joe wanted to grab it back, to pull her into his arms, but he simply watched her get up and walk to where Aaron was still feeding the gulls.

This trip to the beach had been a good thing. Something had changed between them. Louisa might think they were becoming friends again, but Joe suspected it was something more.

Or that it could be something more.

The sun sank below the horizon, leaving a pink tinge in its wake.

When the bread ran out, Aaron came running back to the blanket.

"Aaron, your father and I wanted to ask you about something." She shot Joe a look.

Like old times, he knew what she was thinking. She was going to talk to Aaron about changing his last name. He wasn't sure if this was the time. Aaron had just started warming up to him and—

Louisa continued. "When you were born I didn't give you a name for almost a week. I knew you were Aaron. Aaron Joseph. But I couldn't decide if I should give you your father's last name or mine. Finally, I decided on mine, mainly because it would be easier. But your father's back and he's not going anywhere. Not ever. He's a part of your life now. Nothing's going to change that. And we talked." She looked at Joe.

"Listen, Aaron, this is totally up to you. Your mom and I agreed. If you want, I mean, I'd like, but I'd understand…" He just couldn't think of how to phrase the question so a seven-year-old would understand.

Louisa smiled at him, then at their son. "When you want—if you want—we can change your name to Aaron Joseph Delacamp. It's up to you."

"And neither of us will be mad no matter what you decide."

"I can change my name?" Aaron asked.

Joe nodded.

"Hey, maybe I'll change it to Peter. Like Spiderman. Or Bruce, like Batman, or—"

"Your last name," Louisa said with a laugh. "Because if you were going to change your first name it would have to be something like Goof. Yes, if I were naming you today, I'd totally go with something like Goofball Clancy. Or Goofball Delacamp.''

Aaron giggled. ''Nah.''

''How about Stinky Boy?'' Joe asked, knowing that Louisa was turning a tough decision into something fun.

''Stinky Boy would be a good name for a superhero. Stinky Boy to the rescue,'' Louisa said.

''Yeah,'' Aaron said, his eyes alight. ''Stinky Boy never takes a bath. He just stinks the bad guys to death.''

''Yes, Stinky Boy would be a good superhero,'' Louisa said with a laugh. ''And accurate. It's time to go home. You need a bath.''

She let the question of Aaron's last name wait as they all packed up their impromptu picnic, laughing about Stinky Boy's superstink powers.

Yes, Joe realized, he and Louisa had turned a corner. He wasn't sure where it would take them, but he was sure that he was looking forward to finding out.

''The pizza party's this weekend,'' Pearly said.

''I was just going to pop in after work and then pop out,'' Louisa said.

''Nonsense,'' Pearly said. ''You bring Aaron and Joe. The Five and Dine is closing down Saturday night. Susan is ordering pizza, so even her staff has the night off. The whole of Perry Square will be there. Libby's even bringing the baby. He's a real cutie.''

"But—"

"I already talked to Joe," Pearly said, "and he said it was fine with him if it was fine with you."

"But—"

"So, about seven."

"Pearly," Louisa moaned, even though she knew moaning wasn't going to do her any good.

The woman was a story-telling steamroller. Crushing every argument that stood in her path.

"Louisa, it's just a party," Pearly said with a *tut*. "A party we had planned for a while. It's not a reception, though I still think we'll be planning one of those soon enough. It's just a great opportunity for your friends to meet your son's father."

"Fine," Louisa said, throwing up her hands in defeat. "You win."

Pearly laughed. "I never doubted that I would."

Louisa didn't know how to handle the people on Perry Square. They were a tight-knit community. A family. And when she'd moved The Chocolate Bar here, they'd taken her into their fold, making her one of their own.

During her youth she'd had Joe. Then she'd had Elmer and Aaron.

It wasn't as if she couldn't connect with people. But this sense of family, this bond of the people who worked on Perry Square, she still didn't quite know how to handle it.

"Did I ever tell you about Buster McClinnon?" Pearly asked, cutting into her thoughts.

Despite the fact she felt as if she was being forced into this party, Louisa couldn't help but smile.

"No, I don't believe you have."

"He thought he was all that and then some. A big track star. But one day he planted a kiss on me, underneath the mistletoe. I guess he thought he could outrun me if I got annoyed, but I showed him."

Despite herself, Louisa laughed and said, "What did you do?"

"I chased him all right, chased him out into the hall away from the party and then…"

"Then?" Louisa asked.

"I kissed him back." Pearly grinned.

"Guess you showed him."

"You're darned tootin'. I ruined him for other women."

"So what happened to Buster after that?"

"Don't know," Pearly said with a soft smile and

a faraway look in her eyes. "We graduated, went our separate ways. But now and then I think about him and those kisses. They were pretty special."

Pearly gave herself a little shake. "That's not why I told his story. I simply wanted to point out that I tend to win, so of course I won about the party. I like winning."

"Really?" Louisa asked, with sarcasm practically dripping from her voice.

"And I like it when people obey." She turned to leave. "And, Louisa, you might want to come visit me at Snips and Snaps before the party. I'll give you a trim, and Josie will do your nails up real pretty. As a matter of fact, I'm putting your name down for Saturday at three-thirty so you'll be in fine shape for the party. Don't be late."

Louisa got home that night and told Joe and Aaron that they were apparently all expected at the party.

"I'll see Meg!" Aaron yelled. "I better go practice my signs."

"Signs?" Joe asked.

"Yeah," Aaron said. "Meg can't hear with her ears, so she hears with her eyes. We have to talk on our fingers. Mom taught me the alphabet, but I don't spell too well, so I've been learning words, too. Mom bought a bunch of books. And Meg doesn't get mad when I goof up. She helps me. But I'm going to go practice.''

He ran out of the room.

"Well, he's obviously excited," Joe said with a smile. "Too bad his mother looks like she's on her way to the guillotine. Come on, Lou, it should be fun."

"Yeah, fun," Louisa repeated, though she knew there was a decided lack of enthusiasm in her voice. "I moved to Erie looking for a sense of anonymity, something we never had in Lyonsville. Then I move the store to Perry Square. It's like living in a small town all over again…everyone knows everything about everyone."

"And you still don't want people to know about me?" he asked.

"Would you get over yourself, Joseph Anthony Delacamp," she said, using his full name just like she used to when she was annoyed. "Despite what you think, this isn't about you. It's about me. I don't like being the center of attention. I feel awkward, I feel just like I did back in Lyonsville, as if I won't measure up."

She shrugged, "It doesn't matter. I'll deal with it."

"Lou, I'm sorry."

"Not your problem. It's mine. I've worked so

hard at moving beyond that time. I put this mask on every day and pretend I'm a confident, successful businesswoman and a good mother. And I've pretended so long that sometimes I believe it. But every now and then a small crack shows through, and I realize that no matter how much I pretend, Clancy's kid from Lyonsville is still in there hiding out.''

"Well, Clancy's kid has no reason to hide. She's grown into a pretty amazing woman."

Louisa felt her cheeks warm. "Thank you. And if you're going to be my cheering section let me return the favor by saying that you've grown into a pretty amazing man."

"Thanks."

Joe reached out and traced the line of her jaw with his forefinger.

It was just a featherlight caress, but it shook Louisa in ways she could never explain.

Her first instinct was to draw back, to try to keep the distance between her and Joe. But instead she moved forward, stepping into his arms. "Hold me for a moment, okay?"

She'd barely gotten the words out of her mouth when his arms engulfed her, pulling her into his embrace, pressing her face against his chest.

Louisa drank in the scent of him, basked in the familiar warmth. Years might have passed, things may have changed, but not this, not this feeling of coming home, of belonging.

"Louisa," he whispered before he kissed her.

Soft and sweet, his lips pressed to hers.

And though she knew she should pull free, knew this would only complicate an already complicated situation, Louisa kissed him back. What started out soft and tender quickly escalated, becoming hard and demanding. And in that kiss she rediscovered what had been missing for so long...her heart.

Chapter Six

"Meg!" Aaron cried, minutes after they walked into the party that Saturday. "Meg!" He forgot the little girl couldn't hear him.

Still calling her name, he ran across the room and Joe could see his fingers flying.

Aaron had taught Joe the alphabet so he could say hi to Meg when he met her. "I want her to meet my dad," he'd said.

It didn't get old—hearing Aaron refer to him as "my dad."

Joe mentally reviewed the signs for "Hi, my name is Joe," because he didn't want to disappoint Aaron.

He glanced at Louisa. Too bad she didn't look as excited as Aaron did.

He smiled. "Hey, lighten up. I promise not to embarrass you."

"Why would you think I was worried about that?" she asked sharply.

Too sharply.

"If not that, then what? Because it doesn't take a private eye to figure out that you're nervous."

She offered him a small smile.

"It's a party, Lou. Nothing to fret about."

"Easy for you to say. You went to parties since your childhood. Let's just say that the Clancy family didn't get invited to many."

"Then you have some lost time to make up for." He gave her a friendly elbow to the arm. "Smile. Have fun."

She stretched her mouth to a bad impression of a smile. "How's that?"

Joe shook his head. "You know you can be a bit difficult at times, don't you?"

He didn't have time to continue arguing with Louisa. Elmer and Mabel walked toward them.

"Have you seen Pearly yet?" Louisa asked them.

"Speak of the devil," Elmer muttered. "Come on, Mabel, you can chat with Joe later. I see some-one we have to talk to across the room."

"Doesn't he like Pearly?" Joe asked.

"Of course he does. It's just that they had a fight last time over whether dark chocolate or milk chocolate was better. It got a little heated."

"Which did Elmer like?" Joe asked.

"Dark. And—"

Pearly interrupted. "Joe, Louisa, you made it."

"We're here," Louisa said, her fake smile in place.

Joe smiled and said, "Thanks for inviting me."

"Our pleasure. Let me introduce you around." Before she led him off she said to Louisa, "Nice hair."

"Thanks. I found this terrific salon that does great cuts. Unfortunately the stylist is a bit bossy."

"But smart. It's the perfect cut." She turned back to Joe. "Don't you think?"

"Louisa looks beautiful," he said, and was rewarded by seeing her blush.

"Now, stop flirting with your woman and come with me. There are people to meet. Lou, maybe you could go in the back and give Susan a hand with the pizzas?"

Louisa didn't look as if she was sure she should leave him with Pearly, but finally she nodded and headed into the back.

"That girl's wound tighter than my Aunt Via's

bobbins,'' Pearly muttered as they both watched her work her way toward the diner's kitchen door.

"She's nervous."

"She doesn't like parties most of the time," Pearly agreed. "We've dragged her to a few, but tonight is especially rough on her."

"She's afraid I'll embarrass her," Joe said, wondering just what Louisa thought he was going to do.

"No she's not, you lug head. You got it turned around. She's afraid she'll embarrass you. She's afraid that we'll all see the two of you together and assume you're a couple."

"We are a couple...of sorts, at least." Figuring out just what sort of couple they were was the puzzle.

"For how long?" Pearly asked.

"I'm not leaving." He would never be the one to leave.

"No, I mean how long will you be satisfied with just an 'of sorts' relationship?"

He shrugged.

Pearly simply stared at him, and not sure why he felt compelled to answer her, he finally said, "I don't know. But I don't think Louisa and I can have anything more than an 'of sorts' relationship until we settle the past."

"And she's not in a hurry for that?" Pearly pressed.

"She'll talk about Aaron, about the here and now, but when it comes to what happened, she seems to feel we've said all that needs to be said."

"And you don't?" Pearly asked.

"No. I mean I understand what she's saying, and maybe I don't know her like I once did, but I know there's more. There's something she's not telling me."

"Give her time. She knew a boy, a boy on the cusp of manhood. Let her get to know the man and learn that she can trust you. She'll tell you what you need to know if you don't rush things."

"I'm trying. It's just been hard."

Pearly didn't say anything. Didn't offer up some story about relatives she left behind in the South. Instead, she gave his hand a quick squeeze and said, "Come on."

Over the next half hour she introduced him to almost everyone in the room.

Joe realized early on that he would never manage to remember all the names and who worked where. But there were a few who stuck out.

He would remember meeting Libby and Josh Gardner. They had a new son. Seeing Libby holding the baby on her hips, Joe was hit again with a longing for all he'd missed.

He kept trying to put the past behind him, but it kept intruding, even now, at a party. He looked at the small boy and felt an intense wave of regret that he'd never known Aaron at that age.

"His name's J.T.," Libby said. "Joshua Taylor Gardner."

"I say that's an awful lot of name for something so small, so he's simply J.T.," Josh said.

The baby squealed. "He might be small, but he's got a big set of lungs," Libby said with a laugh. "Excuse me while I go see to His Majesty."

"That was nothing. You should hear him when he's really upset," Josh said to Joe, but the man's eyes were following his wife and son as they left the dining room. "Maybe I'd better see if she needs help."

Josh stuck out his hand. "It's nice to get to meet Aaron's father. I hope we see you around."

"You will," Joe assured him as they shook.

Yes, Josh would be seeing him because Joe wasn't going anywhere.

He scanned the crowd, looking for Aaron or Louisa.

Seeing the Gardners together, so happy, made him

need to connect with them both, to reassure himself that they were there. But he didn't need to go looking for them. Aaron came running over.

"Dad, Dad, this is my friend, Meg." His hands gyrated as he made the introduction. "Do it like I taught you," Aaron prompted.

"Hi. My name is *J-O-E,*" he fingerspelled, thought a moment and continued, *"D-E-L-A-C-A-M-P."*

Slowly the dark-haired girl replied, "Hello. I'm *M-E-G."*

She was older than Aaron, but still very much a little girl. She continued to sign, slowly.

"She said, did you see her baby brother?" Aaron translated.

Joe nodded.

He'd caught the sign for baby, mimicked it and fingerspelled, *"C-U-T-E."*

She laughed and nodded.

Pearly called Joe.

Aaron heard her and said, "Better go, Dad. Pearly gets mad if you don't listen."

"I might not have known her that long, but I already know that annoying Pearly isn't a good idea." He laughed, then smiled at Meg, pointed to Pearly and waved goodbye as he headed back across the room.

"Joe Delacamp, this is our newest married couple, Donovan and Sarah," Pearly introduced.

"Pleased to meet you," he said.

"Where are you working on Perry Square?" Sarah asked.

"I don't actually work on the Square. I'm an E.R. physician at the hospital."

"He's with Louisa," Pearly added. "Over at The Chocolate Bar. They're a couple. You know, love is in the air here on Perry Square."

She paused a moment and said, "Wow, I'm such a poet. Do you think maybe the PSBA could do some advertising near Valentine's Day and use that? Love is in the Air on Perry Square. Hey, I like that. What do you think, Joe?"

"Well, it does rhyme," he answered.

Donovan laughed. "Joe, you're the master of diplomacy. You sure you're not a lawyer?"

"Positive," he said.

"So, you and Louisa are together. That's so romantic," Sarah said with a small sigh. "How long have you two been dating?"

Should he try to explain they weren't really dating, or should he simply answer how long? How long? Would he count the fact he'd known her all her life, or count from the time they'd become a

couple in school, or count from the time he'd rediscovered her in Erie?

He wasn't sure how to answer, but before his silence could reach the embarrassing point, Louisa
stepped out of the kitchen and waved at him.

"It was nice to meet you both, but I'm being
called. Maybe we'll have a chance to talk again
later."

He hurried over to Lou. "You saved me."

"You were looking a bit desperate," she said
with a small laugh. "Since I know the feeling, and
I know Pearly, I thought I'd rescue you."

"My hero. Do I have to offer you a trinket to
show my gratitude?" he teased.

"I figure I owe you more than just a rescue, now
and then," she answered with a smile, but there was
a sense of seriousness in her eyes.

"Lighten up," he said.

An older woman, whom Joe thought he'd met but
couldn't quite identify, started calling Louisa.

"So, do you still maintain that parties are fun?"
she asked as she started toward the woman.

"When I'm with you," he said simply.

She looked flustered by his answer. "I'd better
see what Mrs. Wagner wants."

She took off like a shot and Joe let her go, content
for the moment to hide out in the corner where no

one could ask him awkward questions and from where he could simply watch Louisa as she moved around the room.

Despite the fact she claimed to dislike parties, she circulated from group to group, talking, laughing, animated.

The old Louisa would never have managed it. This new, adult version looked as if she was born to mingle, at least now that she'd warmed up a bit.

He watched how people smiled when she approached. This whole little community on Perry Square liked her, welcomed her.

Joe could certainly understand that. Being with Louisa again...well, sometimes it was easy to forget that eight years had gone by. It felt so natural...so right.

He scanned the room and saw that Aaron was still chattering away at Meg, trying out his newly learned signs. The girl laughed and corrected a few. He felt a sense of pride that Aaron was working so hard to communicate with Meg.

His son was a great kid. Lou had done a great job raising him on her own.

He scanned the crowd and found her again. She was standing with Elmer and Mabel, laughing at something.

"Have some pizza, boy, and stop mooning

around, making gaga eyes at her,'' Elmer called over to him

Pearly was at his side thrusting a plate at him. ''Thanks. And for the record I wasn't, nor have I ever, made gaga eyes at anyone.''

''You're welcome, and you most certainly were making gaga eyes at Louisa.''

Pearly was quiet for a moment, and Joe took a big bite of his pizza.

''Does she know?'' Pearly asked abruptly.

Joe tried to swallow, and started choking.

''Know what?'' he asked when he got his breath back.

''How you feel?''

''Of course she does. We're becoming friends again. We have a son together and are working together for his benefit.''

Pearly snorted.

Then started chuckling.

And soon that gave way to out-and-out laughter.

''Ah, so she doesn't know,'' she said when her bout of hilarity had died down. ''After all, if you're not admitting how you feel to yourself, then how are you going to admit it to her? You might want to rethink that, though. You let her slip away once before and don't want to let her get away again.''

''She's not going anywhere.''

Joe was sure of that. She wouldn't walk out on him again. She wouldn't do that to him, or to their son.

"Not physically, but you both made mistakes before by not being honest about your feelings, about your fears. You can't make that same mistake again—letting your fears keep you from saying what needs to be said."

He wasn't afraid of anything and started to tell Pearly that, "I—"

But she cut him off. "How about I volunteer to take Aaron tomorrow? I'll take him to lunch and a movie."

"Why—"

"Why would I do that? Well, I don't have any other man beating down my door, so I guess poor Aaron will have to do. That, and because I think his mom and dad could use some time alone together."

"Pearly, you're trying to matchmake," he accused.

She just grinned, looking terribly pleased with herself. "Sure I am. And I'm pretty good at it, if I do say so myself. Why, I practically threw Josh and Libby together. And it was one of my stories that pushed Sarah and Donovan together. Heck, if I ever give up doin' hair, I could hang out a matchmaking sign."

"You may be disappointed if you're counting on Louisa and me." There was so much history and baggage between them. He just wasn't sure if they could move past it all.

"I disagree. I'd say you and Louisa are a pretty safe bet."

"I—"

Pearly interrupted yet again. "Did I ever tell you about Fanny Mae and Milton?"

Joe smiled. She was obviously as addicted to storytelling as Louisa had said.

"Just the other day," he reminded her.

"Well, let's just say that what you and Louisa have is as clear as Milton's warty nose was to everyone."

"Pearly—"

"Just tell Louisa I'm taking the boy tomorrow. I'll be there at eleven," she said, and started to walk away.

"What if she has plans?" he asked.

Pearly turned around and winked. "She does. With you. She just doesn't know it yet."

Louisa was bustling around the kitchen the next morning. She'd survived the party…barely.

Being around that many people in a social environment wore her out, though she did just fine at work.

Joe had crawled out of bed much earlier than most days. He looked more than a bit rough around the edges.

"Hey, Aaron," he said as he sipped some coffee, "Pearly wanted to know if you'd like to spend the day with her?"

Louisa turned around, ready to protest, but before she could, Aaron said, "Oh, cool. When's she coming?"

Joe glanced at his watch. "I think she said eleven."

"Man, I better get dressed. That's in just a few minutes," Aaron cried, already halfway down the hall before Louisa could protest.

She kept smiling until Aaron was out of sight. The moment he was gone, she let the fake upturn of her lips slip. "Joe, you can't just go making decisions about Aaron without talking to me first."

He set down his coffee mug with a loud clunk. "Do you consult me about every decision you make about him?"

"No, of course not," she said. "But that's different."

"How?" He sounded almost annoyed, which

made no sense since she was the one who was annoyed.

"It's different because I'm his mother. You have to ask—"

"And I'm his father," Joe interrupted.

"Yes, but..." She couldn't think of a convincing argument to that. She was shut down before she even started.

Joe was right, he was Aaron's father. They might not have a formal agreement, but their arrangement constituted a joint custody, of sorts.

"You didn't have any plans, did you?" he asked softly.

"No," she admitted.

She took a huge gulp of her own coffee and felt the scalding liquid sear her throat the whole way down.

"You trust Pearly, right?" he pressed.

"Yes," she admitted.

"So, what's the problem?"

"Nothing." She hated that he was right. She had no cause to be annoyed. She'd made decisions for Aaron without consulting Joe.

"You're right." She punctuated the admission with a huge sigh. "We're both going to have to be careful to consult each other. I'm just used to doing things on my own. I have to adjust to consulting someone else.''

''And I'm not used to this whole father business, so you'll just have to give me a chance to settle in.''

''Deal.''

She raised her coffee mug in a mock toast, and Joe clinked his against it.

She took a more cautious sip this time.

''Since Aaron's leaving soon, and you already admitted you didn't have any plans, I wondered if you'd like to do something?''

She choked on the coffee.

''What?'' she asked, setting the cup down with a loud clunk, sure that she'd heard him wrong. It almost sounded as if he was asking for a date.

''I don't know. Just something. Together. With me.''

''I—''

Before she could come up with an argument, he added, ''Please?''

Any attempt to get out of doing something with him would sound churlish after that. ''Fine,'' she said.

''Oh, don't gush so much, Lou. You're going to give me a swollen head.''

She laughed, despite the fact she didn't want to.

"I'd be too late. Your head's already way too big. It always was."

He was still sputtering at her teasing insult when she asked, "So what do you have in mind?"

"Just leave it to me," he said.

He was grinning a grin that left Louisa wondering if leaving it to him was wise.

And a small part of her didn't care.

She was spending a day with Joe.

That was enough.

Joe bided his time, finished his breakfast, then walked slowly down the stairs to Elmer's, at which point he hurried because he was feeling quite desperate.

"Elmer, I need help," he said as he rushed into the downstairs living room.

He'd pretended to have an idea about what to do with Louisa, but in truth he didn't have a clue.

"I'll say you need help," Elmer muttered, but a hint of a smile softened the statement.

They weren't exactly friends, but over the past weeks had begun to build a foundation that might someday lead to a friendship.

Oh, Joe didn't delude himself.

If he in any way hurt Louisa or Aaron, Elmer would turn on him. But since he didn't plan on hurting either of them, he felt rather confident that the friendship they were building would last.

"Seriously. Pearly's taking Aaron for the afternoon, and Louisa has agreed to do something with me. The only problem is, I don't have a clue what to do with her."

"What kinds of things did the two of you used to do?"

"Oh, you know, kid stuff. We hung out, saw movies, went to a few dances, watched television together. We were just *together*. It didn't really matter."

"So what's wrong with just being together today?"

"That's what I want, but I want something for us to do while we're together."

"You don't know much about women, do you?"

Joe wanted to retort that obviously he didn't, since he'd already lost the only woman he'd ever loved once and didn't want to see it happen again. But he didn't say it; he just shrugged.

"Do the kind of thing you used to do, forget all your troubles for one day and just have some fun. You two keep circling around the past, so maybe it's time to forget it for a while and look at the present. This is where the two of you always dreamed about ending up, so enjoy the fact that you're both here. There's a great putt-putt course on the bayfront. Go up on the Bicentennial Tower. Eat ice cream. Maybe take a drive out to Waldemeer.''

Joe smiled. ''That's good.''

One day.

One day with no guilt or recriminations about the past. One day just to be Joe and Lou again.

''Yes, it is good if I do say so myself.'' Elmer's chest puffed out a bit.

Joe laughed. ''Thanks, Elmer.''

''Just don't screw it up,'' he said.

Joe planned on doing his darnedest to see to it that he didn't.

''It's a surprise,'' Joe said as he drove down State Street.

''Come on, Joe,'' Louisa protested.

She'd been roped into this excursion. She'd have got out of it if she could, but there didn't seem to be any way to back out. It wouldn't be so bad if she at least knew where they were going so she could prepare herself.

''You know I don't like surprises,'' she said.

''Yes, you do,'' Joe argued, with maddening certainty. ''You just think you don't like them. Sit back and enjoy the scenery. How long has it been since you just sat back and enjoyed a day?''

"I enjoy my life, Joe," she snapped.

At least, she'd enjoyed the quiet pattern of it all until recently.

Joe had thrown her well-ordered world into chaos.

"Okay, wrong question. How long has it been since you took a day off and just relaxed?"

"Relaxing around you is difficult," she answered honestly.

Joe sighed a huge, put-upon sigh. "Lou, you're bound and determined to make this difficult, aren't you?"

"Yeah, I guess I am," she said, grinning despite herself. "When I was young I wanted to make things as easy as possible, but I'm older now and have found that 'difficult' is very often better."

"You're insane."

"Yes I am."

Insane about you, she thought but didn't say. She watched him as they drove.

They drove a few moments in companionable silence.

A sort of peace settled over her.

Even after all the time they'd been apart, he still did something to her, still touched some part of her no one else had ever reached.

Someplace she'd never wanted anyone else to reach.

"My parents come home next week," he said out of the blue.

Her moment of peace was shattered. "Oh."

He stared straight ahead, not even glancing in her direction. "I'm going to call and tell them about Aaron as soon as they're back."

About Aaron.

Not about her.

Louisa knew that Joe was here, was with her, for Aaron's sake, and yet, hearing it put so succinctly stung.

"Okay," she simply said, mainly because she couldn't think of anything else to say.

"I was thinking about making a trip down to Lyonsville to see them."

She wanted to shout, *No*.

She didn't want his parents anywhere near her son. She trusted that his mother wouldn't say anything about why Louisa left. It wouldn't be in her best interests, after all, and his mother was always looking out for her own best interests. But still, there was a small piece of her that was nervous about what new monkey wrench his parents would toss into their somewhat precarious relationship.

But rather than telling him no way was her son going near his parents, she said, "If you want."

He glanced at her, and she saw the troubled look on his face.

"Really," she said, offering him a tight smile. "They're his grandparents, he should know them."

He was back, staring at the road, clenching the steering wheel. "I shouldn't have brought it up now."

"Sure you should have."

"No. That's not what today is about. No more serious talk. We're not here for anything remotely deep and meaningful. We're going to have fun if it kills us. And let's start with…" He pulled into the small lot next to the Harbor View Miniature Golf Course.

"Putt-putt?" Louisa asked.

"We used to play it a lot. I thought it might be fun."

"Fun for me," she said, more than willing to take one day off, just one day with Joe and no serious talk.

One day to just enjoy being with him. "I mean, I always liked putt-putt since, as I recall, I always won."

"I think your memory is faulty, because I remember you as the big putt-putt loser."

"Want to put your money where your mouth is?" she challenged.

"What do you suggest?" Joe asked.

"Loser buys the winner ice cream."

"You're on."

Louisa couldn't remember a time she'd laughed so much.

True to his word, Joe didn't bring up his parents again. As a matter of fact, the deepest discussion they had was whether shooting through the water and making a hole-in-one qualified for the one-stroke penalty for leaving the course.

"Loser," Louisa whispered as she licked her chocolate-and-vanilla-swirled ice-cream cone.

"Cheater," Joe answered back.

"Hey, even if I hadn't docked you a penalty, you would have lost."

"But only by one point," he said.

"One point, two points, ten…it doesn't matter. You lost. Just like you always used to."

"You know, you didn't used to gloat this much," he said.

"Ah, there goes that faulty memory again. Must be a sign of your advancing age, this memory-loss problem. I used to gloat even more than this, and you pouted about the same. I guess some things never change."

"And some things do."

She was silent then, remembering all the things that had indeed changed.

He reached out and touched her shoulder, ''Hey, that's not what I meant. What I meant is, here we are, in Erie, just as we always planned. Finish your cone. I want to go up to the tower and look at the lake we dreamed about for so long.''

His hand fell away and he smiled, ''Come on, lighten up.''

''You're on,'' she said.

They finished their cones and took the elevator to the top of the tower.

Standing at the railing, Joe slipped an arm over her shoulder.

Louisa didn't pull away. Couldn't have pulled away.

His arm felt right.

''We didn't exactly take the path we talked about, and yet, here we are,'' she whispered.

''The lake is as beautiful as I imagined.'' He paused a moment, ''And so are you.''

Louisa could feel the heat rushing to her cheeks. ''I'm average at best.''

It was an old argument.

Joe's next line was exactly what it would have been eight years ago. ''Definitely nothing average here.''

"You're biased," she said. "Because you—" She stopped short.

Her next line would have been, *because you love me*.

But that was eight years ago.

"Because I'm the mother of your son," she said instead.

Joe didn't argue with her change of the script, but he pulled her just a little bit closer.

Love.

It was a word neither of them used. Too much time had gone by and they would never use that word again when referring to each other.

For a moment Louisa felt a sharp pang of regret, but she brushed it aside and concentrated on simply enjoying the day.

"So, are we still in the having-fun mode?" he asked.

"What do you suggest?"

"Elmer said that it's the last weekend for Waldemeer to be open. What do you say we head over and I take you on the Ferris wheel? He says it's an awfully big one. Maybe we'll get stuck at the top and I'll have to comfort you, because you'll be so afraid."

"Ha," Louisa said with a cross between a scoff

and a chuckle. "As I recall you're the one who's afraid of heights. I'll have to comfort you."

"I can live with that," Joe promised. "You'll have to hold my hand and whisper sweet, comforting words in my ear until I forget that I could fall to a certain death."

Laughing, they headed toward the elevator.

Even before stepping into the car, Louisa felt herself falling and feared that if she didn't stop herself she would hit the ground with a thud.

Chapter Seven

Sunday had been magic.

Joe winced as he thought the word.

It was much too mushy for a real man to use, but try as he might, he couldn't come up with a better word, so he was stuck with *magic.*

He figured as long as he didn't use it out loud, he was okay.

But he kept thinking it Sunday. And here it was Monday. He'd rolled out of bed, and his first thought was about seeing Louisa.

"So, what do you say we go meet your mom at the store?" he asked Aaron when he picked him up.

He was picking him up every day at school and

Aaron didn't seem to mind it. As a matter of fact, there were times when Joe thought his son looked forward to those moments as much as he did.

"Sure," Aaron replied. "And then we can stop for McDonald's on the way home."

"McDonald's?"

"Yeah. They've got this cool new truck in their Happy Meals. Justin got one and—"

"You want one, too," Joe filled in.

"Yeah," Aaron said with a wistful sigh.

"Well, we'll have to ask your mom, but I think I could manage to spring for McDonald's for dinner."

Aaron threw his arms around Joe's waist and hugged him tight for a moment. "Thanks. The truck, it…"

His son continued to prattle about the truck and his day at school, but Joe was still reliving the impromptu hug.

He reached out and mussed Aaron's hair and was rewarded with a quick grin.

He felt as if he was on top of the world.

No, take that back, on top of the Ferris wheel again. Elated and able to do anything.

"Let's go get your mom," he said, anxious to have the three of them together again.

It was a great day.

* * *

It was a day from hell, Louisa thought.

One of the Murphy's Law sort of days where anything that could go wrong did go wrong.

She needed to make more Mud Pies. They were selling like hotcakes, and her stock was low. Elmer was supposed to come in and help her, but he'd called to say he wasn't feeling well. So she was trying to juggle customers and chocolate making.

This was one of those days she wondered why she had thought opening her own store was such a good idea.

She started to fill the small chocolate tank from the larger tank in the back room. Tubing carried the chocolate from one to the other. It was a great system.

The bells over the front door jingled.

She stuck her head through the door, ready to shout she'd be out in a minute, when Aaron rushed in, a small whirlwind of motion. She met him halfway.

"Mom, Mom, can we go to McDonald's for dinner? Dad said he'd treat, but we had to ask you. They're giving away trucks with the Happy Meals, and Justin got one and it's so cool and I need one and— Can we?"

"You said it was up to me?" she asked Joe.

He grinned. "Well, we talked about consulting each other, so there was no way I was saying yes before asking you."

He was teasing. She saw it in his eyes and grinned. "Thanks. But I'd say this is a case where I don't have a chance in the world of saying no. I mean, we can't have poor Aaron go another day without his truck, can we?"

"That's what I thought," Joe said, trying to maintain a serious face.

"Yay!" Aaron cried. "I love McDonald's. I want a milkshake, though, not pop," he told Joe. "I always get chocolate milkshakes, and Mom always gets strawberry. What about you?"

"I get ice tea."

"Boring, Dad," Aaron told him.

"Yeah, that's me. Your boring dad."

Louisa saw how moved he was that Aaron had called him Dad.

Tears welled in her eyes, but she blinked them back. She knew she'd let them fall when she wrote about this moment tonight.

Yes, this was a moment that definitely would be immortalized in her journals.

She looked at the two of them and her heart felt filled to the point of bursting.

Filled.

"Oh, my gosh," she gasped, as she ran into the back room.

"Louisa?" Joe called, following her.

The light on the wall was blinking, and the small vat was overflowing. Chocolate ran in rivers over the side and onto the floor.

Louisa hurried to the switch across the room. Hurried too fast, without taking into account the fact that chocolate was slippery.

Very slippery.

She skated a short distance, then lost her footing and fell. There was a small chocolaty *gloop* sound as she hit the floor.

"Lou, are you okay?" Joe asked.

"Fine. Could you get that switch?" she asked, pointing to the wall.

Joe started across the floor with a lot more cautious restraint than Louisa had shown. He hit the switch, then turned around, looking rather triumphant.

It was the turn that got him.

Louisa watched him fall in elegant slow motion, his arms windmilling at his side as he tried for balance that never came.

Gloop.

He was down, as well.

"Hey, what about me?" Aaron cried.

With no hesitation, he ran full force toward the chocolate-covered floor, stopping abruptly as he hit the sweet mess, and literally skating across the puddle to the other wall.

"Ha. I didn't fall."

"Aaron Joseph, you get off the chocolate while you're still clean," Louisa scolded as she cautiously got up. "I've already got as much mess as I can handle."

"But it's fun. It's like ice-skating, only with chocolate. Justin thought he was so cool with his truck, but wait till tomorrow. I'll have a truck and I can tell him I went chocolate-skating. No one else ever got to do that."

"Aaron, enough. Get off the chocolate, then slip off your shoes and go get me a bucket."

"Aw, Mom."

"Now."

Aaron used a skating sort of gait and started back across the lake of chocolate.

Louisa looked at Joe, who was slowly climbing to his feet. "I'll help clean up."

"You don't have to. The rule here is, If you make the mess, you clean the mess."

"Ah, but maybe the rules should be, If you have a problem, you call on me. And vice versa. I'm here for you, Lou, even when it's only a bit of chocolate on the floor." He looked at the floor and chuckled. "Okay, so maybe this qualifies as more than a bit."

She got up and looked at the mess. "Yeah, I guess it does. I got distracted when the two of you came in, and then Aaron called you Dad and my heart melted. Chocolate was the last thing on my mind."

She paused and looked at the chocolate-covered man in front of her. "I'm so happy for you."

She could see a myriad of emotions in his eyes as he said, "For us. I'm happy for us."

"Hey, here's the cleaning stuff. I'll help, Mom." Before she could say no, her ever-helpful son was skating across the chocolate again, this time in his socks with a big bucket in his hand.

It must have been the bucket throwing off his balance, because suddenly Aaron was falling into the chocolate. But unlike his parents, he bounced right back to his feet, grinning from ear to ear as he licked at his chocolate splattered face. "Cool."

Louisa looked at her two chocolaty guys and thought, if all her messes ended up being this much fun, her life was going pretty well.

Louisa smiled.

She realized she'd been smiling since the chocolate cleanup. They'd all ended up such a mess, but it wasn't the mess she remembered, it was the fun.

They'd laughed as they'd scooped up the sticky chocolate.

Aaron kept calling Joe "Dad" and every time he did, she and Joe exchanged a look. She knew what he was feeling. It was like old times, but better.

The chocolate incident had marked a significant turning point in their relationship.

Something had changed in that one afternoon.

The difference was there…palpable.

It wasn't as if the past eight years had been erased. They were still there, standing between them. But it was as if something new was growing around the pain…something that had been a mere bud eight years ago and was finally sprouting.

Louisa knew that Joe realized it as much as she did. It was there in the way he looked at her—quiet looks that felt like coming home.

He was becoming more and more a part of their lives.

Louisa was accustomed to sharing a cup of coffee with him in the morning before she went off to work and he went to bed.

She was getting used to coming home and having dinner waiting for her.

Her heart melted as Aaron gradually began to call Joe "Dad" on more and more occasions.

Watching the two of them grow closer was a dream come true.

Joe had joined their nighttime routine.

After dinner, before bed, they all three read together, sitting on Aaron's bed. Occasionally Aaron would sit in the middle, wrapping an arm around both Louisa and Joe as she read.

This imitation of a real family was what she'd always dreamed about. But she knew it was just that, an *imitation*.

Despite the fact they were growing closer, there was still a wall between them.

Each moment, each occasion, was stored away.

She'd learned the hard way that the good times could disappear in just the blink of an eye. She didn't doubt that Joe would be there for Aaron, but she couldn't quite believe he'd be around for her; so each little gesture, each tender stolen kiss, was stored away.

She wrote each treasure down in her journal, needing to have something tangible to remember them by.

Thursday night the phone rang and she stopped scribbling, glancing at the clock before she picked it up.

Ten o'clock.

Who called at ten o'clock at night?

"Hello?" she asked.

"Hey, Lou."

She smiled as she set down her pen and curled into her pillow. "Joe. What's up?"

"It's slow tonight. I was thinking about you and just wanted to hear your voice."

"As it so happens, I was thinking about you, as well."

Every night, as she wrote in her journal, she thought of him. Every entry for eight years had started with "Dear Joe."

This quiet time each night had always been their time, even if he hadn't known it.

"Oh, you tell me what you were thinking, and I'll tell you what I was thinking."

There was suggestive teasing in his voice that made her smile.

"I was thinking you're still the most conceited man I know and I refuse to share my thoughts with you for fear your swollen head won't fit through the doorways."

"Really?" he asked. "You were thinking stuff that would make me that conceited? Ah, Lou, you always did have a way with sweet words. Ask me what I was thinking."

She chuckled. "What were you thinking, Joe?"

"I was thinking you're still the most beautiful

woman I know. And I don't worry about you getting too conceited. Sometimes I worry that you'll never see yourself the way I see you."

The conversation had shifted and Louisa knew that rather than engaging in playful banter, Joe was serious.

"I see myself honestly…the way I am."

"No," he argued. "You've never been able to do that. You've always weighed your self-perception against everyone else's opinion."

"I used to, but not anymore."

"So, when I say that you're the most beautiful woman I've ever met…that I'm in awe at what you've built for yourself and our son here…that with every day that passes I realize just what a great job you did with Aaron, you can take the words as the truth and just accept them?"

"Well, I'm honest enough to argue the 'most beautiful' part," she maintained.

"No other woman has ever looked as beautiful to me as you do."

She blushed at that. Blushed from the tips of her toes to the roots of her hair.

"Beautiful or not, I will graciously accept your praise for the store. I'm proud of The Chocolate Bar and wouldn't argue with you about that. But about

Aaron, he's the way he is simply because he's an amazing kid. We both did that. Good genes.''

"Loving. That's what it is, Lou. We both know how rare a good mother can be. You've given him something neither of us ever had. You gave him a happy, loving home.''

"Thank you,'' she said, though it was difficult to squeeze the words past the emotions that were clogging her throat.

Though she'd tried to assure herself that she was past needing anyone else's approval, Joe's words meant something to her.

Needing to lighten the tone, she said, "This isn't what you really called for, is it?''

"I just wanted to hear your voice and thought I'd call and say good-night.''

She wasn't sure what to say to that, so she settled for a simple, "Oh.''

Joe chuckled and tsked. "This is where you're supposed to say you wanted to hear my voice, too, and you're glad I called.''

"I did. I am.''

"Things are changing.'' His words echoed her own thoughts. "We need to talk about what it all means.''

"Let's not and say we did. I don't want to spoil this…whatever this is that's happening.''

"We can't go on like this forever."

"For a while longer."

"Okay. A while." There was something in his tone that told her a while was all she had left.

"Listen, I've got to get some sleep if I'm going to be able to function tomorrow. See you in the morning."

"Good night."

She was pulling the phone away from her ear when he said her name, "And Louisa?"

She pulled the phone back. "Yes?"

"Sweet dreams."

She smiled as she hung up, then grew serious.

Yes, things were changing. She thought she and Joe were growing closer. But there was one thing standing between them, one last omission.

She knew that she'd had the best of intentions when she hadn't told him everything.

When she hadn't thought there was any future for her and Joe, she'd felt comfortable not telling him the whole story of her departure. It would have served no purpose to drive a wedge between him and his mother. But now, as they grew closer, that omission stood between them, weighing on her.

She should tell him.

She didn't want any more secrets between them. If she'd been honest eight years ago, if she'd shared her doubts and fears, maybe so many things would be different. But she couldn't live her life on what might have been. She needed to go forward.

Should she tell him?

She didn't know.

"Mom, Dad, I want to talk to you," Aaron said the next day at dinner, the picture of seriousness.

Joe wanted to mess his hair or say something funny to make the boy smile. Making Aaron smile, making Louisa smile. Those were moments Joe lived for.

"Yes?" Louisa asked.

"Uhh," Aaron said, dragging the word out for a long time, as if working up to something. Then in a quick rush of words, he said, "You said I could think about changing my last name?"

Joe felt a solid mass lodge itself in his throat as he nodded. "It's up to you."

"I thought and thought about it. Me and Elmer talked about it even, and I want to, but not now."

"Oh." A wave of disappointment washed over Joe, but he forced a smile and said, "That's fine, Aaron. Whenever you want to, or if you never want to, it's up to you. We said that and meant that. I mean it. Your last name won't change the fact that I'm your father and I love you."

"Do you want to talk about why not?" Louisa asked gently.

Aaron frowned. "'Cause if I changed my name to Delacamp, you'd be the only Clancy left, Mom. Joe's not the only Delacamp. My grandma and grandpa are, too. It's not fair to leave you all alone, Mom."

"Honey, I don't mind." She took his hand and pulled him onto her lap.

If the conversation wasn't so serious, Joe would have laughed. Aaron didn't quite fit the way he must have when he was younger…bits and pieces dangled off, but neither of them seemed to mind.

Louisa brushed aside a stray piece of Aaron's hair and said, "As a matter of fact, I think you should."

"Why?" Aaron asked, voicing Joe's question.

"Because you are your father's son, and that means you should share his last name."

"But you're my mom. Maybe you could change your name to Delacamp, too, then we'd all be the same."

"I don't know if that will work, sweetie," she said hedging.

"How about we give your mom some time to think about changing her name, and then we'll all talk about it again," Joe said, his voice husky with emotion.

"Yeah. It's a big thing and it took me a long time thinking," Aaron said. "So you take your time, Mom."

"Thanks, honey," she said.

"Okay," Aaron said, obviously feeling as if things were settled. "I'm going down to see Elmer. We're tying some new flies for fishing."

"Go on," Louisa said.

They both watched their son sprint out of the room.

"Thanks for stalling and giving me some time to think about how to answer him," Louisa said.

She gazed after Aaron, a worried look on her face.

"I wasn't just stalling," Joe said. She turned around and faced him as he continued, "I think you should think about it."

"Change my name to Delacamp?" she asked.

"I did ask you to marry me." They hadn't talked about marriage for a while, not since things had started to change.

"You asked me because I had your son. Because it would be convenient. Being married to me would make the whole who-gets-Aaron question easier."

He hadn't realized he'd been holding his breath until he let it out with a whoosh.

He'd wanted her to simply say yes.

He hadn't expected it, but he'd wanted it all the same.

"We can't live here with Elmer forever. We need to come up with a better solution. Marrying me would be better," he maintained.

"I don't think so," she said stubbornly.

"But—"

"Listen, Joe. I saw my parents' marriage, a marriage that was built on many things, but never on love. I won't settle. Not even for Aaron. I deserve more than that."

Her answer tore at him.

Part of him wanted to say, I love you, I've always loved you. It was the part he'd buried eight years ago when she'd left.

He'd had to suppress that part or he'd have lost his mind. He wasn't sure if he was strong enough to let it go now, to take the risk of loving her and losing her again.

"So what are we going to do?" he asked. The question was as much for himself as it was for Louisa.

"One problem at a time. Right now I have to think of a way to answer my son."

"Our son," he reminded her.

She reached out, took his hand and gave it a quick squeeze. "Yes. Our son."

"So, we're back to just waiting and seeing."

"After eight years, a little more waiting won't hurt us," she said.

Joe wasn't sure. Wasn't sure if he could wait longer, wasn't sure if he could tell her how he felt, wasn't sure exactly what he felt.

Basically he wasn't sure of anything except that her hand felt right in his.

He squeezed it and said, "We'll wait a little longer."

Chapter Eight

Waiting wasn't something Joe was good at.

By Saturday morning he'd already done enough waiting. He wanted… He wanted what he'd always wanted, to build a family with Louisa.

Maybe they weren't in love the way they'd been all those years ago, but they had a firm foundation for a good relationship.

They respected each other.

They were becoming friends again.

They had a son together.

That was enough, Joe told himself.

He fingered the ring in his pocket. It was a sapphire. He'd been looking at diamonds, but this ring's stone had caught his eye.

The sapphire was the exact color of Louisa's eyes.

He'd laid out all the logical reasons why they should marry.

He had feelings for her. He wasn't quite sure how to identify them. They were different from the ones he'd felt when they were younger, but they were real, and he knew he could be a good father and husband.

He just had one more thing to do before he asked her to marry him.

He had to tell his parents about Aaron and about the fact that he wasn't going to stop asking Louisa to marry him until she said yes.

Elmer was right: part of the problem before was the fact he'd kept Louisa hidden away. He hadn't forced his parents to choose…accept Louisa or lose a son.

But now he would.

He'd grown up, he realized. He didn't need his parents' approval any longer.

All he needed was his family…Aaron and Louisa.

He placed the call from down at Elmer's. Elmer was out again with Mabel, and Joe had the privacy he needed.

He dialed the number.

"Hello?" his mother said.

"Mother. It's Joe."

"Joseph. I'd hoped you'd call. We had a lovely time on our trip. Why—"

He interrupted, knowing she could go on for a long time about the trip. He didn't want to hear her name-drop, didn't want to hear every move they'd made.

He needed to say what had to be said. "Mother, I need to tell you something. I found Louisa."

There was complete silence on the other end of the phone.

"I found her," he repeated. "And I'm going to marry her."

"After the way she left you?"

"She's explained everything. She was pregnant. She had my son and then there was—"

"She's lying."

Of all the things Joe thought his mother might say as he told her about his son, this didn't even come close. "What?"

"I said, she's lying. Whatever she said about me, it's a lie."

"Mother, Louisa doesn't lie," Joe said, giving the most vague response he could think of.

He wasn't sure what was going on and wanted to keep his mother talking. He felt a spike of dread climb up his spine.

"Joe, it was for your own good, don't you see?"

There was something in her voice that Joe had never heard before.

It sounded like desperation.

She continued in a rush, "You were going to medical school. You were going to make something of yourself, and that girl would have ruined all of that, would have ruined your life."

"What did you do, Mother?" he asked softly.

"You know. But it's not like she said, I swear. I just had a little talk with her. My only concern was for your future."

"And…?"

"Listen, she could have stayed, could have told you. Instead she took my check and left. She couldn't get out of town fast enough. That tells you the kind of woman she was…is."

"You bribed her?"

Louisa had taken money from his mother? How could she not have told him? What was going on?

A coldness swept over him…. He felt almost numb with it.

"No, I simply suggested it might be better for all parties concerned if she left. I gave her money for her living expenses. She waited until the money I gave her ran out and then came with her hand out to you for more. Well, don't you give her a thing,

Joe. Not another dime. By the time our lawyers are through with her—''

''Aren't you even going to ask about your grandchild? The child you tried to hide from me?''

''Now, don't you use that tone with me. I'm still your mother.'' Gone was the desperation. In its place was his mother's normal sense of superiority.

''His name is Aaron.'' Enunciating, he said slowly, ''Aaron Joseph Clancy. But not for long. Soon it will be Aaron Joseph Delacamp.''

''Don't do anything hasty, Joseph,'' she said. ''Our lawyers—''

Joe ignored her and continued, ''He looks just like I did at his age. He's smart…he's so smart. And funny. He wasn't thrilled to see me at first, but he's getting used to having me around. He calls me Dad.''

''You shouldn't get too emotionally caught up with the boy.''

''He's my son, Mother. That means something.''

That bond—parent to child—was something his mother wouldn't understand. She'd never been overly maternal. She was more concerned about the family name than about the family…about him.

''It's biological, nothing more,'' she said.

That one statement summed up his mother's views.

"Maybe that's why we have the relationship we do. You see me as a biological issue instead of an issue of the heart. Aaron is everything to me, Mother. Everything."

"And *that girl?*" That same hint of scorn was in her voice as she said those words, *that girl.*

"That girl has a name. Louisa."

"Louisa," his mother spat out the name as if it were something vile. "What is she to you?"

"I don't know. There's so much I don't understand, but she's important."

A few moments ago he'd have said, I think I love her, but knowing that she'd kept something this big from him…he just couldn't voice his feelings.

His mother paused a moment and finally said, "I never understood why you'd lower yourself to her level."

"If there was any lowering, it was on her part."

"She didn't mind reaching out and grasping that money."

"I don't understand everything, but I do know if she took your money—"

"If? You think I'd lie?"

"Yes." Joe hated to admit it, but there it was. "You'd lie if it suited your purposes. I know that. I've always known that. But not Louisa. If she did take your money, I know it wasn't for herself, but rather for our son." He paused. "My son."

"Joe."

"I planned to ask you to come visit, but I think that should wait until I figure out what's going on here."

"The lawyers—"

"Aren't necessary," he said. He wasn't clear about everything, but that much he knew. "And, Mother?"

"Yes." Her voice sounded weary, old.

"When, and if, you do come to visit us, you're going to have to accept Louisa, because I might not know much, but I do know that she's a part of my life. After this conversation, I'm not sure in what capacity, but she's the mother of my child, and as such, you will treat her with respect."

"Joe—"

"Goodbye, Mother. I'll talk to you soon."

Why hadn't Louisa told him that his mother knew? That she'd given her money? Why was she holding that back, and what else wasn't she telling him?

"Hey, guys," Louisa called as she entered the quiet apartment. No answer. Maybe they'd gone out somewhere. She tossed her bag in the entryway and kicked off her shoes.

What a day. Although she had help on Saturdays, she'd gone in for the morning to do some busy work and had been just that—busy.

"Louisa?"

She jumped.

Joe was sitting in a dark corner of the living room.

"I'm beat. How was your day? Where's Aaron?"

The urge to walk over to him and throw herself on his lap, to be held and cuddled, was overwhelming. It had been a long, busy day and only the thought of coming home to Aaron and Joe had kept her going.

"Long day?" he asked.

There was something in his voice…a coldness she hadn't heard since that first day in the candy shop.

"What's wrong? Where's Aaron?"

"Elmer took him out to McDonald's for supper. We need to talk." That flatness in his voice made her blood run cold.

"Sure," she said, amazed that her voice sounded so normal.

She walked over to the couch and sat opposite Joe.

As she studied him, she could make out how haggard his face looked. She wanted to reach out and touch him, to soothe away whatever was troubling him. Daily the need to touch him, to connect with him, to simply be with him grew. How long could they go on like this?

"What's wrong?" she asked.

"I talked to my mother today."

"Yes?" Just thinking of Helena Delacamp was enough to make her blood run cold.

"What did you do with the money, Louisa?"

"She told you?" Louisa couldn't keep the surprise out of her voice.

She'd counted on Joe's mother's sense of self-preservation to keep her from saying anything.

"Yes. What did you do with it? She claims you were a gold digger, that you took the money she offered you and ran with it."

"I did."

"That's it. That's all you have to say for yourself?" he asked.

So cold. His voice was so cold. The distance between them wasn't physical. He was pulling back from whatever bonds they'd managed to reestablish.

The loss of that connection hurt like a physical pain.

"What more do you want me to say?" she asked. "Your mother's right, I took the money she offered. And if put in that situation again, I'd do the same."

How could she defend herself against the accusation? She had taken the money. Every cent of it.

And she'd do it again in a heartbeat.

"I want the whole story," he said. "I've known you were holding something back, but this? I want to know why you didn't tell me my mother knew you were pregnant. I want—" He stopped short.

"Yes?"

"Just tell me."

They'd been building something. Even if Louisa hadn't wanted to talk about it, there had been something there, something in the way he looked at her. But it was gone now. His face was a blank mask.

She willed herself to be strong.

"I was going to tell you about the baby, just like I said. But then there was the engagement announcement, and I didn't know what to say. I knew you never wanted children, I knew I wasn't good enough for you, but still I was going to tell you. Then one afternoon your mother came by...."

Louisa's heart clenched as she remembered that afternoon. She'd been scared before, but Mrs. Delacamp's visit had crushed her.

"She told me that she wanted me to leave, to let you have the life—the wife—you were destined to have. She said all the things I felt in my heart," she admitted. "Then I blurted out I was pregnant."

"And?" His voice more gentle now, even though it remained distant.

She wasn't sure she would ever be able to span that distance.

"She said everything I feared you'd think. It was as if she could read every one of my secret thoughts and fears. She said that I was trying to trap you. That I would ruin your life. That you'd end up hating me for everything you lost because of my mistake."

"And you believed her?"

"Joe, it wasn't her saying it, it was my thinking it. I believed all that before she opened her mouth. Despite my fears, I still would have told you, but then…"

"Then?" he asked.

"Then she told me if you married me they'd cut you off without a dime. There would be no medical school. If you were with me, she'd take away your dream. I'd be responsible for taking away your dream of becoming a doctor. You'd lose everything. How could I do that to you? I already worried that I wasn't good enough, that you'd end up resenting me. But if you lost all you'd worked for? I—"

She shook her head. "I wasn't strong enough then to stand up to her, to stand up for myself, for us. Now? Maybe I could take the chance that somehow we could make it work. I've changed a lot over the past eight years. But then? I couldn't.''

He sat there, just looking at her.

She could see his pain. He practically vibrated with it.

More than ever she wanted to reach out across the space that separated them, not just the physical space between the couch and his chair, but across all the years she'd given away. Eight years without him. She wanted to span that time and make things right.

But she couldn't.

Suddenly she remembered something. ''Wait a minute, I have something for you. It won't change anything, but maybe it will explain it better.''

She went into her room and searched through her desk until she found the small bankbook. She took the eight journals that lined her shelf, then went to her nightstand and took out the most recent one. She carried it all out into the living room and placed it on Joe's lap. ''Here.''

''What all this?'' he asked, looking at the pile of books on his lap.

''This is the bankbook. All the money your mother gave me went into a trust fund for Aaron. I never touched a cent of it. Even when times were tight. It was a matter of honor. If nothing else, I need you to know it wasn't for me."

She nodded at the journals. "And these…I always meant for these to come to you. I started a journal when I discovered I was pregnant, and started a new one when Aaron was born. It became a tradition. Each year on his birthday I started a new one. They were always meant to come to you."

He opened one and read aloud, "'Dear Joe…'" then snapped the book shut. "Why wait until now to give them to me?"

"They talk about that meeting with your mother. I didn't want to tell you that part of it. You've always had such a rocky relationship with your parents and I wanted to spare you that. In the end, telling you about your mother's visit wouldn't have changed anything. I was the one who made the decision. I was the one who left."

"You didn't want me to know that my mother sent you away?"

Louisa shook her head. "She didn't send me away. I ran away."

He stood. "I've got to think."

He was going to leave and there was nothing she could do.

"I understand," she whispered.

"I don't see how you understand, since I don't have a clue."

She reached out and laid her hand on his arm. He pulled away and her heart twisted.

"Think what you will of me," she said, "but don't let this taint the relationship you're building with Aaron."

"Even now you still don't trust me?"

She'd heard pain before, but now there was anger. "What?"

"You still think I'll walk away from him or hurt him. If you can think that, then you don't know me at all. Maybe you never did."

He turned and left the apartment.

Louisa sank back into the couch. She couldn't think. She just stared at the door and waited.

He'd taken the journals.

She hoped they'd give him some measure of comfort.

Feeling as if she was moving in slow motion, Louisa wrapped her arms around her legs and simply sat in the semidark room, waiting.

Joe didn't know where to go...didn't know what to think.

He couldn't stay in the house, couldn't go to Elmer's. So, he drove, the notebooks piled on the passenger seat. He drove around Erie, around the town they'd always dreamed of moving to.

Aimlessly he drove down State Street, past Perry Square, to the bayfront. The Bicentennial Tower stood at the end of the dock, a huge reminder of what he thought he'd been rebuilding with Louisa.

He didn't stop. He looped around the dock and headed back up State Street, then turned west on the Bayfront Highway.

Finally he knew where he was heading.

He drove to the peninsula, to the farthest beach, and parked. He took the top two notebooks and got out. The wind was raw and bitter as it blew from Canada across the lake, but Joe barely registered it as he sat on a weather-beaten picnic table and stared out at the water.

The waves were wild, crashing over the stone barriers that had been erected to stop erosion.

The sky had late-autumn clouds, puffy and white, hiding the sun, which would occasionally break free and shine as it dipped closer to the lake.

Joe reached for the oldest book, not sure he was ready to look at it, to see the girl from his past, a girl he thought he knew but maybe never had. A girl who'd walked away from him and from his love.

"Dear Joe," it began. He traced the letters with his forefinger.

He remembered all their hopes and dreams. He would be a doctor, she wanted to work in advertising.

They'd move to Erie, Pennsylvania, where no one would know them. They'd marry and have children…white picket fences.

A dog.

He suddenly remembered, they'd planned on a dog. She planned on getting it from the pound and naming it Rufus. He'd asked why, and she'd said, "Rufus is a good name for a mutt."

She'd laughed then. It was a joyous sound. That's what he'd heard the day in the candy store, that laugh as the three of them had rolled around in the chocolate. He'd heard it that day when she'd beat him at putt-putt.

God, he loved that sound.

He started reading the journals. Every entry started with, "Dear Joe." She wrote of wanting to tell him about the baby, about her fears, about reading about his engagement, about her talk with his mother.

She wrote about leaving Lyonsville and her trip to Erie.

She noted all the changes in her body. The day she'd met Elmer. Working for him in the store. The birth of their son. Her agony over what last name to give Aaron.

Her fears, her hopes, her joy.

Everything.

The past eight years were here.

He finished the two journals and went back to the car for more, but realized it was too dark outside to read them. So he went to the hospital and found an empty room and continued reading there.

He laughed out loud at some of Aaron's antics. He felt his own blood run cold as Louisa described every illness, every bump or bruise.

He learned about Aaron's favorite blue binky, and Elmer's midnight run to find a replacement when it was lost one night. He realized more than ever that Elmer was the father Louisa had never had but had always deserved.

He envied that bond.

He owed the old man more than he would ever be able to repay.

He read of Aaron's first day at school, of the opening of The Chocolate Bar.

He read all of the past eight years.

And though the journals focused on Aaron, there was so much of Louisa in them. The something he'd been feeling for her slowly unfurled, growing, blossoming. And as Joe finished the last book he realized just what the feeling was.

Love.

He'd wanted to say it for a while now but hadn't been sure of it. Hadn't been sure he could truly trust Louisa enough to love her again.

He thought the feeling had died all those years ago when she'd left. But now he found that it had simply gone into hibernation, waiting, biding its time.

Like the wart on Pearly's Milton Hedges's nose, it was so obvious that he couldn't believe he'd missed it before.

He loved Louisa Clancy when they were kids, and he loved her now, though it was a different, more mature kind of love.

Since he'd found her in the chocolate store he hadn't known what to think, what to feel, and suddenly he did.

And he knew why she hadn't told him about his mother's talk, because she loved him, too. She loved him eight years ago, and however misguided, that's why she'd left. She didn't want to hurt his dream of becoming a doctor.

And she still loved him now, which is why she didn't want to hurt him by telling what his mother had threatened.

She loved him.

He loved her.

He left the hospital as the sun was rising, knowing just what he had to do.

"Now, Louisa," Elmer said soothingly.

But Louisa didn't want to be soothed. She was sick with worry. "He's been gone all night, Elmer."

"He's fine. Sometimes a man just needs to go off by himself and work things out."

"What if he's not? What if he's left?" That thought was too terrible to bear. She'd lost Joe once and wasn't sure she would survive losing him again.

"That boy wouldn't leave," Elmer assured her. "Aaron's here, after all."

Yes. Joe wouldn't leave Aaron.

But he'd leave her. He was furious all over again. And who could blame him? She'd lied to him.

Well, not exactly lied, but she hadn't exactly told him the truth, at least not the whole of it.

"But what should I do?" she asked.

"Wait. Give the boy some time to work it out."

"The boy doesn't need time to work it out," Joe said as he walked into Elmer's kitchen. "I've worked it out just fine."

Louisa couldn't tell what he was thinking. His

expression was blank. But still she was relieved to see him.

"Joe?" she said as she looked him over. He looked all right. Haggard. Tired. But all right.

She couldn't quite read the expression on his face. It wasn't anger.

"We have to talk."

Louisa's heart sank. His voice was flat. She couldn't read what he was thinking, but then she didn't need to.

"Fine," she whispered.

"Alone."

"I can go—" Elmer started to say.

Joe interrupted. "No, don't go. As a matter of fact, will you stay and watch Aaron?"

Elmer studied Joe a moment and then said, "Yes."

"Joe, I—" Louisa started.

"Stop," he said. "Just hold that thought and come with me."

"Where are we going?"

"Wait. You'll see."

Louisa was silent. After all, she'd said everything she had to say. Joe knew it all.

Well, maybe not all.

She still hadn't told him how she felt about him.

She gnawed on her lip. This obviously wasn't the

best time to blurt out the words, *I love you. No matter what I've done in the past, that's one thing that never changed. I love you.*

She didn't want to even think about what his reaction would be to such a declaration right now.

They pulled into the parking lot of the Humane Society.

The Humane Society?

"Joe, what's going on?" She looked at the building, completely mystified. "I don't understand."

"We're buying a dog."

"It's Sunday. I think they're closed," was all she could think to say.

Of all the things she'd been ready to hear, all his accusations, all his anger, this wasn't even on the list. "Why are we buying a dog?"

"Because we need one. And next week we'll start looking for houses. Something close to the water," he said.

"We have a house, with Elmer."

"We'll get something with an in-law apartment. If we can't find one, we'll add on. That way if he finds the house lonely, or ever needs us, he'll have a place to go. Because he's family."

She studied the man in the driver's seat. Maybe he'd cracked. Maybe the pressure had finally gotten to him. "I don't understand."

"It's all about family and what makes one. Don't you see? Elmer's family. He loves you unconditionally. He is the father you never had. He's there for you no matter what. I never had that growing up, that kind of unconditional love, at least not until I had you."

He took her hand in his. "You said you didn't feel as if you were equal to my family. You weren't. You were so much more. I wish we'd had these past eight years together, but I understand why you did what you did. You loved me enough to walk away."

"But I was wrong," she said. "I should have told you, should have trusted you...trusted our love."

"Yes, you should have. You didn't trust that I loved you enough to walk away with you. But you loved me then, and you love me now. When I asked you to marry me, you said you wouldn't marry without love. What you didn't say is that you loved me—you still do. You did then, you do now. Which is good because I love you, too."

"But you can't. I left. Too much has happened. I didn't tell you about your mother."

He pulled her closer, wishing he'd really thought this thing through. Sitting in front of a Humane Society wasn't exactly the place to pour out your heart.

But the words wouldn't stay locked up until they were at a more romantic setting, so he said, "Louisa, we're meant to be together. What we have is special and rare, and it's something that time or mistakes can't erase. We love each other. And we have eight years to make up for. So, say you'll marry me, then let's go buy our dog. We'll name him Rufus...."

He remembered, she realized. He remembered her insane chatter about a dog.

Tears were falling from her eyes, but only because she was so full of love it had to overflow somewhere.

She said, "We'll name him Rufus because it's a good name for a dog."

"And we'll buy a house—"

"On the lake. You'll be a doctor, I'll own a chocolate store, and we'll have loads of kids."

He nodded. "That about sums it up."

"Are you sure?" she asked.

He reached in his pocket and pulled out a beautiful sapphire ring. He slipped it on her left ring finger. "I've never been more sure of anything in my life."

Epilogue

"Aaron Joseph Delacamp, keep that dog out of the water...." Louisa let the admonishment fade away since both Aaron and Rufus were already in the water. "He's going to soak the car on the ride home."

Joe just laughed. "I planned for it and packed the car with a ton of towels."

"Smart man."

"Lucky man, Mrs. Delacamp," he murmured as his hand caressed her slightly rounded stomach.

She snuggled closer. Eight months of marriage and she still hadn't shaken the sense of awe that all her dreams had come true.

Even Joe's parents were coming around. They'd visited Erie just last week to meet Aaron. What could have been a strained visit was eased by Aaron's excitement at finally meeting his grandparents. If asked, Louisa would never have guessed what happened next…Joe's parents fell in love. Uncharacteristically, head-over-heels in love with their grandson.

Loving Aaron had given them all common ground—a place to start building a relationship.

"Look, the sun's about to set," Aaron cried, racing toward them with a very wet dog at his heels. "Listen. Maybe we'll hear it this time."

They were all silent. Just as the sun touched the water's edge, Rufus started barking at a bunch of seagulls and chased after them.

Aaron said, "There's always next time," and ran after him.

"Missed it again," Louisa said.

"I didn't," Joe said.

"You heard the hiss?"

"No, you see, you were wrong. It's not a hiss. I heard a beating just as the sun hit the water. It said, Louisa, Louisa, Louisa…just like my heart does."

She laughed and pressed her head against his chest. "I don't hear it."

"Then you're not listening hard enough. That's how my heart has always beaten."

She lifted her head and kissed him. "Have I mentioned I love you lately, Mr. Delacamp?"

"Maybe, but no matter how many times you say it, you can't say it too much."

"I love you," she said.

"Me, too."

Curled in her husband's arms, watching their son and his dog chase gulls as the sun sank below the horizon, Louisa knew that she was living her dream.

A dream that she was pretty sure would last forever after.

* * * * *

Don't miss Holly's next book,
HOW TO HUNT A HUSBAND,
from Harlequin Duets in September 2003.

Only love could renovate the hearts
of two rough-and-tumble architects!

#1 *New York Times* bestselling author

NORA ROBERTS

brings you two classic riveting tales of romance.

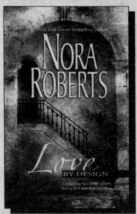

BY DESIGN

Containing LOVING JACK and BEST LAID PLANS

And coming in October, watch for

LAWLESS
by Nora Roberts.

Available at your favorite retail outlet.

Where love comes alive™

If you enjoyed what you just read,
then we've got an offer you can't resist!

Take 2 bestselling love stories FREE!

Plus get a FREE surprise gift!

It's romantic comedy with a kick
(in a pair of strappy pink heels)!

Introducing

HARLEQUIN®
flipside™

"It's chick-lit with the romance and happily-ever-after ending that Harlequin is known for."
—*USA TODAY* bestselling author Millie Criswell, author of *Staying Single*, October 2003

"Even though our heroine may take a few false steps while finding her way, she does it with wit and humor."
—Dorien Kelly, author of *Do-Over*, November 2003

Launching October 2003.
Make sure you pick one up!

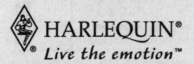

HARLEQUIN®
Live the emotion™

Visit us at www.harlequinflipside.com

#1684 LOVE, YOUR SECRET ADMIRER—Susan Meier
Marrying the Boss's Daughter

Sarah Morris's makeover turned a few heads—including Matt Burke's, her sexy boss! But Matt's life plan didn't include romance. Tongue-tied and jealous, he tried to help Sarah discover her secret admirer's identity, but would he realize *he'd* been secretly admiring her all along?

#1685 WHAT A WOMAN SHOULD KNOW—Cara Colter

Tally Smith wanted a stable home for her orphaned nephew—and that meant marriage. Enter JD Turner, founder of the "Ain't Getting Married, No Way Never Club"—and Jed's biological father. Tally only thought it fair to give the handsome, confirmed bachelor the first shot at being a daddy…!

#1686 TO KISS A SHEIK—Teresa Southwick
Desert Brides

Heart-wounded single father Sheik Fariq Hassan didn't trust beautiful women, so hired nanny Crystal Rawlins disguised her good looks. While caring for his children, she never counted on Fariq's smoldering glances and knee-weakening embraces. But could he forgive her deceit when he saw the real Crystal?

#1687 WHEN LIGHTNING STRIKES TWICE—Debrah Morris
Soulmates

Joe Mitchum was a thorn in Dr. Mallory Peterson's side—then an accident left his body inhabited by her former love's spirit. Unable to tell Mallory the truth, the new Joe set out to change her animosity to adoration. But if he didn't succeed soon their souls would spend eternity apart.…

#1688 RANSOM—Diane Pershing

Between a robbery, a ransom and a renegade cousin, Hallie Fitzgerald didn't have time for Marcus Walcott, the good-looking—good-kissing!—overprotective new police chief. So why was he taking a personal interest in her case? Any why was *she* taking such a personal interest in *him*?!

#1689 THE BRIDAL CHRONICLES—Lissa Manley

Jilted once, Ryan Cavanaugh had no use for wealthy women and no faith in love. But the lovely Anna Sinclair seemed exactly as she appeared—a hardworking wedding dress designer. Could their tender bond break through the wall around Ryan's heart…and survive the truth about Anna's secret identity?